A Cruising Misjudgement

Elaine K Collier

PEACHY PUBLISHES

Copyright © 2023 by Elaine K Collier

All rights reserved.

No part of this publication may be reproduced, distributed or transmitted in any form or by any means, including photocopy, recording or any other electronic or mechanical methods, without the prior written permission of the author, except as permitted by U.K. copyright law. For permission requests contact the author.

The story, all names, characters and incidents portrayed in this production are fictitious. No identification with actual persons (living or deceased) is intended or should be inferred.

First Published 2023

ISBN: 9798861770552

www.elainecollier.com

Also By Elaine K Collier

Innocents Abroad Crime Series

A Greek Misadventure

A Sardinian Misfortune

A Malaysian Misdemeanour

Non-Fiction

Once Bitten, Twice Prepared

The Bigger Picture

All books are available from Amazon

Chapter 1

"Morning, sugar," said Fiona, watching and waiting as her best friend desperately tried to get her phone upright and her face in view.

"Morning, Fi," Donna replied eventually. "How's it all going?"

"To be honest, Don, I don't know whether I'm coming or going at the moment. I've just about finished packing and this afternoon I've got a meeting with Steve, my boss. I need to check with Michaelis that everything is OK with the yacht and on top of all that Lauren can't decide what she wants to do next so is doing absolutely sod all."

"Oh, not much going on then?" laughed Donna. Although Fiona had a lot happening in her life, Donna could always make her laugh.

"Oh Donna, sorry, didn't mean to go off on one. But that's not the reason I'm phoning. Steve has asked me if I would consider giving a series of talks on a cruise ship. He can't do it so thought I might like to and have a holiday at the same time. Plus, I can take someone with me. You up for it? I have to give him my answer when I see him later."

"Bloody hell, Fi, am I ever! We've never done a cruise, so this will be an amazing new experience. When is it?"

"Not until September so we've plenty of time. We haven't got a holiday planned yet, so this could just be it. I will have to do a bit of work whilst on board, but the talks are only about forty-five minutes to an hour each and not every day, which leaves plenty of free time."

"Where's it sailing to?"

"I've got a feeling it's the Caribbean, but need to check that. If it is, there will be lots of days at sea, but we should get a stop at New York."

"Oh God," exclaimed Donna, "that would be absolutely brilliant."

"Great. Then I'll confirm with Steve and get more information. So glad you're coming, Don. We'll have an amazing time."

"We certainly will. Right, I'd better go now, so much to do at the moment, what with the house move and the wedding, but we'll catch up later. You are still coming at the weekend, aren't you?"

"Oh yes. As you say, lots to do with the new houses. What do you need me to do?"

"We'll talk about it at the weekend and see what needs doing," said Donna.

"OK, babe, see you Friday but I'll talk to you before then."

Chapter 2

Three Months Earlier

Shortly after returning from Malaysia the previous year, Donna received a letter and cheque from Mr and Mrs Raja, the fellow passenger who suffered a cardiac arrest on their flight to Penang. Dave roughly calculated the three million ringgits cheque to be over half a million pounds, but Donna didn't feel it right to accept such a large gift, a bunch of flowers would have been enough. She phoned and spoke to Mrs Raja, who dismissed all her protests, saying the money was peanuts to her and her husband and they both hoped it would bring Donna some pleasure.

Half a million pounds was an amazing amount of money, and it would certainly help with the house project that Dave and the boys were working on. It would also allow her to give up her job if she wanted to. Maybe she could start her own little business, but what would it be? They could certainly afford some wonderful holidays, but Dave's love of travel was pretty much non-existent. Thoughts and ideas were vying for space in her head. Never would she have thought she would have such an amazing dilemma. She immediately phoned Fiona.

"Fiona, I've just got a letter from the man who had the medical emergency on our flight to Malaysia, and they've sent a cheque for about half a million quid."

"Bloody hell, Don, that's unbelievable."

"I know. I've phoned them and said it's much too much money and I couldn't possibly accept it, but they won't hear of it. They're so grateful that Sun Tan is alive and feel that it's the very least they can do."

"What will you do with the money?" Fiona asked.

"I don't know. I've got hundreds of thoughts going round in my head. I'll wait until you're next here and then we can talk about it."

"OK, darling, I'll look forward to helping you spend it."

In the meantime, Fiona had her own two life-changing letters waiting for her. The first confirmed the sale of her house in Oxford; her move to Cambridgeshire was now a reality. The second letter invited her to make an appointment with Harrington and Penn, Solicitors, at her earliest convenience.

The following week she made the trip to London where Mr Harrington informed her that Nikos Laskaris had left her a sizeable amount of money in his will, plus his beloved yacht, *The Angel*. In a daze, she left the office and phoned Donna.

"Donna, I've just left the solicitor's office and Nikos has left me money and *The Angel*."

"Bloody hell! That's fabulous, but what are you going to do with the yacht?"

"God knows. At the moment it's all too much to take in."

"Don't do anything in haste, babe, take your time and really think over your options," said Donna, worried that Fiona might do something totally knee-jerk which she would regret later.

"No, I won't. *The Angel* has such special memories, but what the hell do I do with a yacht in Cambridgeshire?"

"God knows, it will look a bit over the top going up the River Ouse," Donna laughed. "Listen, why don't you come for the weekend and we can go over the options?"

"Yeah OK, sounds like a good plan. I'll come Friday afternoon, if that's alright?"

"Perfect. See you then."

Fiona arrived at Donna's house late afternoon, and it wasn't long before the pair of them were sitting at the breakfast bar in the kitchen, with a bottle of wine and discussing their options around their new-found fortunes. They had just opened their second bottle when Dave walked in.

"Hi Fi, good to see you," he said, giving her a hug and a kiss on the cheek. She was much more of a sister-in-law to him than Donna's own sister, and he loved her to pieces. "Blimey, you two are going great guns," he said, nodding at the second bottle of wine.

"We have a dilemma, babe," said Donna. "I told you that Nikos has left Fi *The Angel*, but the thing is, she's not sure what to do with it."

"The way I see it is you have two choices – keep it or sell it." Dave had always been very black and white where decisions were concerned. You either did something, or you didn't. There were no shades of grey.

"Yes, but it's not that simple, darling. There is a great deal of sentimental attachment to the yacht, but the practicalities of keeping it are immense."

"Not really. Let's take it one step at a time." Dave grabbed a beer from the fridge and sat down. This, he thought, was going to be a long session.

"Fiona, do you want to keep the yacht or sell it?" he asked. "Be truthful now and just give me the first answer that comes into your head."

"Keep it," answered Fiona. "I'm too emotionally attached. Too many happy memories were made on *The Angel* and I couldn't bear the thought of a stranger having it."

"Right," said Dave, writing 'Keep It' on a sheet of paper. "Where will you keep it?"

"It will be easier to keep it in Rhodes, don't you think?"

The questions went on for the rest of the afternoon, but finally the three of them had come up with a plan.

Fiona's first task was to talk to Michaelis, the captain of the yacht, and ask if he would be interested in staying with her and running it as a charter business. What to do next depended on Michaelis' answer, but he jumped at the idea and together they worked out a plan that would ensure a profitable business and also allow the crew to keep their jobs. Plus, she and Donna, along with Dave, Matt and Jason, could spend time on it whenever they wanted.

With the dilemma over the yacht solved, she could now turn her attention to the house move.

Chapter 3

With the house in Oxford just about packed up, Fiona was ready for the move to Cambridgeshire.

When the opportunity to buy a plot of land cropped up, Dave had jumped at the chance and, together with his three boys, had built five homes. His plan was for him and Donna to have a brand new home, the boys would have a house each and he asked Fiona if she would like to buy the fifth house. After careful consideration, she agreed, reasoning that it didn't matter where she lived as long as she had enough space should either of her children wish to come home. Being closer to her best friends was too good an opportunity to refuse. Someone once told her that close friends were relatives of the heart that you choose to have, and this she truly believed. With the exchange of contracts about to take place, she was ready to leave.

However, she had mixed feelings about leaving Oxford, her job and her friends, but her house had never been the happy family home like the one Donna had created. Now she was on the brink of a brand-new start, and whilst she was sad in some ways, she had a lot to look forward to.

"What time do you think you'll be here?" Fiona asked Donna during one of their phone calls.

"Dave reckons that if we arrive mid-morning on Thursday, we can get most of it loaded into the vans and then Friday morning we'll pack any remaining stuff and get on our way."

"Perfect," Fiona replied.

"OK, love, got to go. See you Thursday."

"Love you, babe."

"Love you too."

***

Donna and Dave arrived in the first van by eleven thirty, closely followed by Gavin, Mark and Tom in the second. After a quick coffee, they got to work and by early evening they had the majority of Fiona's home loaded into the vehicles.

"Let's stop now," said Fiona. "I've just ordered pizza and there's beer and wine in the fridge."

"Sounds good to me," said Dave, locking up the van and walking back into the house. "This place looks huge now all the furniture has gone."

"Yes," Fiona replied, "it's a big house, and far too big for just me. The new house will be much more manageable."

"You're not sorry to leave, are you?" he asked.

"Yes and no. I have memories here, some good, some not so. It's where I brought my babies home to, but then they left as soon as they could. There were shit times with Jeremy, and I was pleased when he left. But it's lonely on your own, so no, Dave, I'm fine and looking forward to a new start."

"Good. Let's crack open some beers then."

The six of them sat around the floor at the end of the kitchen, where floor to ceiling windows gave them a view over the beautiful garden that Fiona had created.

"Right," said Donna, munching on a mouthful of pepperoni pizza. "Tomorrow Dave and the boys can load up the remaining stuff and head back home. Fi and I will do any final cleaning and follow on in her car. The priority when we get to the other end is to get Fi settled and at least one bed made up."

"What about your stuff though?" asked Fiona.

"We're OK-ish," replied Donna. "All of our stuff got moved at the beginning of the week, so it just needs sorting and packing away. We've got beds to sleep in and a kettle. Lucy is at their house now and they're getting deliveries of new furniture daily. I think, once we're all there, we can work together and get everything sorted."

"It's quite exciting now it's happening, isn't it?" Fiona smiled, her moments of sadness giving way to the joy of being close to the people she cared most about.

"Yes, it is," replied Donna. "At least we'll all be close together and just a stone's throw away if any of us need anything."

"We'll have some amazing times, I'm sure of it."

Chapter 4

Dave and the boys left Oxford by seven thirty the following morning, and just after nine Fiona shut the front door for the final time.

"How are you feeling, babe?" Donna asked, as they headed north on the A34 towards the M40.

"I'm OK," Fiona replied. "I had a moment when I closed the door for the last time, but now I'm looking forward to a new start, Gavin and Lucy's wedding, and our cruise."

"Oh yeah, I nearly forgot about the cruise. I've not told Dave yet. I wonder what he'll say. I'm so looking forward to having you near me, Fi, no more driving backwards and forwards."

They hadn't gone very far when Donna's phoned pinged with an incoming message.

"It's Matt," she said. "He wants to know where we are."

Hi Matt

Just leaving Oxford and on our way home. Fiona's with me and ready to start her new life.

D xx

Two minutes later Matt replied.

Fabulous, do you need any extra help this weekend?

M xx

"Matt's asking if we need any help this weekend. Is that OK with you?"

"Of course," Fiona replied. "The more pairs of hands the quicker we can all get sorted."

Be grateful for more hands and always love to see you. Haven't got all the beds up yet so bring sleeping bags. See you at the new houses.

D xx

Will do, see you soon.

M xx

"They're on their way to the house now," Donna said. "It will be good to be all together with so much space."

"Yes it will. I love spending time with those two."

"When do you need to start work again?" Donna knew that her friend had got some time off for the move, but she didn't know how long.

"I've got a couple of weeks, and then Steve's agreed to see how it goes. He said he doesn't want to lose me completely so is being very flexible. We'll just have to play it by ear."

"Yes, I'm sure it will all work out for the best."

"To be honest, Donna, I don't need to work now that Nikos has left me so much money. It's more a question of what will I do all day if I don't work? I am not going back to being one of those 'ladies that lunch'."

"I should hope not," laughed Donna. "Don't get me wrong, it's lovely to go to lunch with friends, but when it's a group of women you don't really gel with and they're all vying to be top dog, then that's not right."

"You're right there. I love the work I do with the forensic team, it's just the travelling I don't want."

"You're not regretting the move already, are you?" asked Donna, concerned her friend felt she might have made a mistake.

"Oh God no," Fiona replied. "I know this is the right thing for me, to be much closer to you and Dave will be wonderful. No, I'm happy with the move and I guess it will just take a while to adjust and see where my life is heading now."

"There's no rush, babe."

"What about you, Donna, have you decided what to do with the money the Rajas sent you?"

"No, not really. But one of the things I am considering is giving up work."

"Won't you miss it?"

"Yes and no. Like you, I'm not fond of the commute and Cambridge is a pig of a place during rush hour. But again, it's what to do with my time if I don't work."

"I'm sure we'll come up with something if we're both home all day together."

"I'm sure we will," laughed Donna. "The worrying thing is what kind of plan will we come up with?"

"Here we are," said Fiona as they finally turned into the quiet tree-lined street that led to their new homes in the cul-de-sac at the end.

Five brand new, four-bedroomed, detached houses stood in a crescent, each waiting to greet its new occupier. Fiona pulled into the crescent and followed the road round, past Donna and Dave's house at number one, the three boys' homes and finally to her new home at number five. The two vans were already outside, the boys offloading their contents with Lucy directing operations. Fiona pulled her Mini onto the drive and as the pair got out, Dave appeared at the front door with a bottle of bubbly in his hands.

"Welcome to your new home, Fi," he said, standing back to let Fiona pass. Champagne flutes lined the breakfast bar in the kitchen and Dave popped the cork and filled them. Everyone filed in, welcoming their final resident.

"A toast," he said, raising his glass. "To all of us, our new homes and a brand new start."

"To us," they all said in unison as they took their first sip.

"Room for two more?" came a voice from the open door, and Matt and Jason walked in clutching bags of groceries and other goodies.

"Fabulous," said Fiona with tears in her eyes. "My family is just about all here."

Chapter 5

After a few of weeks of frantic activity, they all finally felt settled in their new homes. Donna found it strange to not have her boys in the house but took comfort in the fact that they were constantly in and out borrowing stuff that never got returned, collecting bits and pieces they had forgotten and even staying for the odd meal.

Fiona cooked for everyone a couple of times a week and they quickly made it a rule that Sunday lunch was 'family' time, and all ate together at either of the girls' homes.

There was still work to be done with the gardens, but they agreed it would be best to leave that until after Gavin and Lucy's wedding. Lucy wanted a marquee in their garden, so it made sense to leave the space un-turfed and unfenced.

Fiona started work again and so far, it was going well. Anything she needed to talk to Steve about she did via Zoom, so there was really no need for her to travel.

Donna decided to transfer to the Cardiac Unit at Hinchingbrooke Hospital in Huntingdon, but was finding it hard to settle in. Working closer to home cut down travelling time, and certainly saved a lot on petrol, but she wasn't sure she had made the right decision. Time would tell, but she always had the option to leave if it didn't become easier.

It was after one particularly rowdy Sunday lunch when Matt and Jason joined them for the weekend, that Donna suggested they should give their crescent a name. Until now they had referred it to as just 'The Crescent' but giving it a name seemed the perfect idea. Through a haze of red wine, everyone threw names into the mix, many of which were downright stupid, but Jason scribbled all viable suggestions down in his notepad.

"There's one name that no-one's suggested yet that I think is meaningful to everyone," Jason said.

"What's that?" asked Matt.

"Angel," he replied.

Everyone went quiet, lost in their own thoughts. Fiona began to cry quietly as memories of happy times with Nikos flooded back. Finally, Donna broke the silence.

"I think that's just perfect. Angel Crescent."

"It keeps Nikos with us," sobbed Fiona. Matt rose from the table to comfort her, tears glinting in his own eyes.

"Are we all agreed, then?" asked Dave, the response unanimous.

"Right, I'll put an application into the authorities first thing in the morning. Our new address will be Angel Crescent."

Chapter 6

The week leading up to the wedding was hectic. The marquee was erected in the back garden, complete with a footpath from the driveway and sturdy flooring so the ladies wouldn't catch their heels and topple over, especially after they'd had a few drinks. A steady stream of people set tables with white and burgundy linens, polished cutlery and gleaming glassware. Beautiful floral centrepieces were added.

The boys hired a helium gas cylinder and spent the day blowing up white and burgundy balloons. Donna had to put a stop to it after she caught them sniffing the stuff and acting stupid.

Matt and Jason arrived on the Friday afternoon and brought Jason's brother Andrew with them. As soon as Donna knew Jason had an older brother, who just happened to be single, she went into matchmaking mode, thinking he might be perfect for Fiona.

Fiona was thrilled that her two children, James and Lauren, were coming home for the wedding. It was the first time they had been to their mother's new home and Fiona hoped they would approve. She also hoped that they would find time to talk properly and their relationship deepen.

The wedding day finally dawned with blue skies and warm sunshine. Angel Crescent saw its residents running between houses, doing final checks in the marquee, and checking that everything and everybody was ready. The cars arrived just before midday. Gavin and his brother Mark, who he asked to be his best man, got into an open top classic car whilst Donna, Dave, Fiona, Matt, Jason and Andrew used a limousine.

The church looked lovely, packed with beautiful floral displays – their perfume wafting out into the congregation. After greeting friends and family, the wedding party made its way to the front pew to await the bride. Lucy was a fashionable five minutes late and looked stunning in a simple figure-hugging white gown with a long train. Gavin stood and moved towards the altar to greet her, Donna and Fiona both had tears in their eyes. The wedding ceremony was beautiful and after standing for what seemed like hours for photographs, they finally got back into the cars and headed home to Angel Crescent and the marquee.

"Thank God that bit went off smoothly," said Donna, after she and Dave welcomed guests and she finally stood with a glass of bubbly in her hand. The rest of the day passed in a blur. The speeches were excellent, and Mark excelled himself with anecdotes of his brother that had everyone crying with laughter. But there's always one guest at every wedding, and it was Lucy's granddad George who stole the show. His hearing aids gave off a constant high-pitched whistle. The screeching feedback with the microphone had everyone wincing and holding their ears, although he seemed completely oblivious to the racket. Dave worried it might attract the neighbourhood dogs. George's dentures were a bit of a problem too, the top set constantly dropping every time he spoke. Eventually, he took them out and dropped them in a glass of water on the table.

"That's better," he declared, with a gummy smile. "Now, who's for a dance?"

Friends of the couple joined them for the evening and the dance floor turned into a heaving, sweaty throng of gyrating bodies. Granddad George was the centre of attention again with his energetic version of The Macarena. In his over enthusiasm he lost balance, grabbed Emma, the chief bridesmaid, for support and ended up taking her down with him. Clutching her tightly to his chest, his lascivious gummy smile made it clear to everyone that he assumed his luck was in. It took three men to prise Emma from his clutches. The guests could see the funny side. A few had set their phones to video, but poor Emma was left traumatised, convinced she would end up on TikTok.

Slowly, Donna began to relax and enjoy the evening, especially as the main part of the day was over. Enjoying a slow dance with her husband was definitely a moment to treasure. Dave didn't dance much so she hoped one of the boys were taking some photos. She noticed Fiona was also enjoying a dance with Jason's brother, Andrew. *Oooo watch this space*, she thought.

What a wonderful day, she sighed with pleasure as she watched her youngest son, Tom, heading towards them.

"Mum, Dad, have you got a minute? Need to have a quiet word."

Chapter 7

Donna wandered out to the garden the following morning with a cup of coffee. Her hangover wasn't as bad as she feared, but that was partly due to Tom dropping his bombshell. That boy certainly knew how to pick his moment. She sat on a bench in the middle of the gardens, quietly reflecting on the day before. Everything had gone smoothly, and Gavin and Lucy were about to leave for a two-week honeymoon to the Maldives.

The catering company would be back shortly to collect their things, and the marquee would be taken down the following day. Everything would soon be back to normal.

Except her baby was leaving home, and she didn't like it one bit. She thought Tom was settled in his own house but after spending most of the previous day talking to James and Lauren, he suddenly announced that he was off to see the world. She didn't want him to go and sat imagining all the horrors that could befall him.

"Morning, Auntie Don, you look deep in thought." Lauren had wandered over from her mother's house and perched next to Donna on the bench.

"Morning, darling," said Donna, looking round and smiling at her. "You're up early this morning."

"Yeah, couldn't sleep, too much on my mind. But why are you looking so glum? The wedding was a huge success."

"Yes it was, wasn't it." Donna smiled as she thought about the previous day. "Oh it's not the wedding, sweetheart, that was a perfect day. I guess I'm feeling a little down after Tom's announcement last night."

"It's the best thing he can do, a year out travelling is a fantastic opportunity and so much experience to be gained. I wouldn't have missed mine for the world."

"I suppose so. I guess this is how your mum felt when you took off."

"Do you think so?" asked Lauren. "I thought she was glad to see the back of me."

"Is that what you really thought?" Donna asked incredulously, as Lauren slowly nodded her head. "Let me tell you, young lady, your mother was in pieces the day you left. She didn't want you to know in case it spoiled your enjoyment or stopped you from going, but she worried about you every second of every day you were gone. It wasn't the best time in her life either, what with your father and everything. It was a time she could have done with the support of her children, but she wanted to support you and encourage you to find your own path."

"I didn't know," said Lauren, tears glistening in her eyes.

"There's a lot about your mum that you don't know. But one thing is for certain, never, ever doubt her love for you. She's like a lioness with her cub, she would kill for you," said Donna, giving Lauren a hug. "You, young lady, are the daughter I never had, and I worry about you too. You are loved very much by all of us."

"Thank you," Lauren whispered.

"Now then, tell me what's kept you awake half the night."

"Oh, it's nothing really, just trying to decide what I want to do with the rest of my life."

"I wouldn't call that nothing, it's a big decision to make. Have you got any ideas?"

"I think I want to be a therapist of some sort."

"What, like in massage therapist?"

"No," Lauren laughed, "more like a talking therapist. I love finding out about people, what makes them tick, why they do the things they do."

"Not unlike your mum then?"

"Yes and no. Mum solves crimes, but I want to help make people better. I want to help them rebuild their lives after trauma, to be strong and happy again."

"Oh Lauren, that's amazing."

"Do you really think so? I think Mum will be OK with it, but not sure about Dad."

"Darling, this is your life, you get to choose. You're right, your mum will be fine. Your dad is a different kettle of fish entirely, but do you need his permission to do something that makes you happy and will help a lot of people?"

"No, I don't do I?"

"I suggest you do your research, find out what it entails and then ask yourself if you still want to do it."

"Thank you," said Lauren, jumping up from the bench and giving Donna a hug before making her way back to the house.

"Promise me one thing," she called to the retreating back, "talk to your mum before you make any decisions."

Lauren turned and gave her the thumbs up and a big smile.

Donna sat back and lifted her face up to the warmth of the sun, lost in her thoughts about how quickly the children had all grown up.

"Morning, babe, what you doing out here on your own?" said Fiona ten minutes later, coming from the opposite direction with a cup of coffee of her own.

"Morning, sugar. I couldn't sleep so I'm just sitting here mulling over yesterday."

"It was a fabulous day, wasn't it?"

"Yes, it was. You seemed to get on well with Jason's brother."

"Yes, he's really nice, nothing not to like really. But you seem a bit down this morning, and I'm certain it's not just because the wedding is over, so what's up?"

"Oh Fiona, you know me so well. Tom's leaving. He dropped the bombshell last night."

"What do you mean, leaving? Leaving for where?" Fiona asked, puzzled.

"Basically, he wants to take off travelling for a year. He feels too young to be stuck here in his house, and wants to take off and see the world."

"Can't blame him for that, Donna, it will be a fantastic experience for him. But I completely get how you feel about it. I was the same when James and Lauren took off."

"He spent most of the evening chatting to James and Lauren and I think listening to their experiences tipped the balance."

"He'll come back, you know."

"I do know, but I've always had my boys with me and I'm not ready to let go. He's my baby."

"I know, darling, but we don't get a choice in what our kids do when they grow up. We have to let them go and just let them know that we'll always be there for them. When he comes back, you will have your boys close to you again."

"You're right of course, and I have to wonder when you got so wise," Donna laughed. Fiona put her arm around her friend's shoulders and gave her a hug.

"All will be well, you'll see. So what's he going to do with the house now?"

"Says he wants to rent it out, so he's got some income to fund his trip. Makes sense, but I don't fancy strangers moving into Angel Crescent, do you?"

"No, not really." Fiona thought for a while. "Actually, I've got an idea."

"Steady, babe, it's far too early in the morning for good ideas."

"I know," laughed Fiona. "But Matt and Jason are looking for somewhere to live, what if they rented it?"

"Oh God, Fi, what a brilliant idea. That would be just about perfect. I'm sure Tom would sooner someone he knows takes it rather than having strangers in his home. Let's go and ask them." Donna jumped up from the bench.

"Shouldn't we wait until they're up?"

"No time like the present," said Donna, making her way across to Tom's house, where the couple had stayed overnight.

Chapter 8

In less than an hour the deal was done.

Matt and Jason didn't take long to accept. They both agreed that it solved their current house hunting problem. It didn't matter to Jason where in the country he lived, but Matt would have further to travel if he were to remain with the airlines. Perhaps it was also a good time to think about a complete change of career, but he had no experience in anything other than working as cabin crew.

Delighted that he would get a regular monthly income, Tom knew the pair would look after his home. He hot-footed it off to his friend's house to plan their travel itinerary.

Dave and the girls were happy as having Matt and Jason living in Angel Crescent would maintain their close-knit family group.

"Right," said Dave, "why don't we all head down the pub to celebrate? We can get some lunch there too to save you girls from cooking."

"Oi you, less of this saving you girls from cooking," said an indignant Donna. "What's wrong with you blokes doing Sunday lunch?"

"Nothing at all, my little pigeon," said Dave, wrapping his arms around his wife and kissing the tip of her nose.

"Is Andrew up yet?" Fiona asked Jason. "Perhaps he would like to join us too?"

"I'm sure he would. I'll go and get him."

"Oooo you and Andrew, eh?" laughed Dave. "I saw you both getting a bit down and dirty on the dance floor last night."

"Well, he's a nice guy and we can't leave him out, can we?" said Fiona, trying to justify why she wanted him to come along. Although why she had to justify it, she had no idea.

"Come on, sugar plum," said Matt, taking Fiona's arm. "Here comes the other two so let's get going."

They found a table for six easily enough, and Dave got a round of drinks in. They each ordered the carvery and sat back to enjoy their drinks before they rushed to collect their food.

"At least the wedding's over now and everything went well. Now we can all relax a bit," said Donna.

"Yeah, we can for now. One wedding down, two to go," said Dave.

"There is one thing," said Donna, thinking that now was a good time to tell Dave about the cruise.

"What's that, love?" asked Dave.

"Fi has been invited to give a series of talks on a cruise ship in September and she's suggested we use that as our annual holiday."

"Oh God," said Dave, running a hand over his face. "You certainly know how to spoil a perfect day."

"It will be fine this time, Dave," said Donna. "We're on a boat, what could possibly go wrong?"

"Famous last words, babe. You were on a boat in Rhodes, but you both managed to get yourselves kidnapped off it."

Dave had a valid point. Wherever the two girls went on holiday, they always managed to get caught up in something shady. Admittedly it was not always of their own making, but Donna could not seem to walk away from anything she felt was wrong. Although a cruise ship had to be safer than some places they had visited, and had good on-board security, he wouldn't bet money on them not finding something to involve themselves in.

Chapter 9

"Ready, Fi?" Donna called, opening the door to her friend's home. Dave had pulled the car around the crescent and was waiting outside Fiona's house, ready to put her luggage in the boot.

"Coming," she answered, wheeling a large suitcase outside and turning to lock her front door. This was the first time in years that she had left her home without worrying about what she might find on her return. They had a hidden safe in the back garden containing all their keys, giving access to all the houses if needed, so she knew her home would be looked after, plus she never had to worry about forgetting her keys. They lived in a good area where properties were fairly safe and Dave was also talking about installing electric gates at the entrance to Angel Crescent. Donna joked about living in a gated community, but she knew he had a valid point if the level of crime were to increase.

With the two girls and all their luggage finally in the car, Dave set off for Southampton. It took almost three hours before they reached the outskirts of the city, but the journey had on the whole been good. Southampton was a different matter. Following the signs as best they could, they seemed to turn this way and that before they finally drove into the ship's terminal and the drop-off point.

As soon as the car stopped a porter appeared at their side with a trolley. He unloaded their luggage and told them the next time they saw it would be in their cabin.

"Don't worry, we'll be absolutely fine," said Fiona as she turned to Dave and gave him a hug goodbye.

"I know, but I still have to remind you to keep out of trouble."

"We will, darling," said Donna, as her husband's strong arms engulfed her. "I may not message every day, depends on where I can get a connection and Wi-Fi on board is bloody expensive, but I'll do it as often as I can."

"OK, darling, but please promise me that you won't get yourselves involved in any trouble."

"I'm sure there won't be anything to get involved in," Donna laughed, but raised her eyebrows at Fiona over his shoulder.

"Have a great time and I'll see you in a couple of weeks. Love you."

"Love you too, darling. Have a safe journey home."

Dave got back into the car and drove off as Donna and Fiona linked arms and made their way into the terminal building.

Chapter 10

Opening their cabin door, the decor and comfort of what was to be their home for the next couple of weeks pleasantly surprised Fiona.

"I like this," said Donna, looking beyond the twin beds that dominated the room. "I'm surprised we have a sofa and coffee table. Oh look, there's a bottle of bubbly and a couple of glasses.

"I like it too," replied Fiona. "I'm surprised by how spacious it actually is, and I'm sure I can find a home for everything."

"I'm sure you will," laughed Donna.

"Bathroom's tiny," called Fiona as she opened the door and poked her head in.

"Blimey," said Donna, joining her at the door. "You can sit on the loo and brush your teeth at the same time."

A knock on the door heralded the arrival of their cabin steward and their luggage.

"Good afternoon, I am Bernard," he said. "I am your cabin steward so anything you need, please just ask or you can call me. Your luggage has arrived."

Bernard pulled their cases into the cabin and lifted the first onto the plastic cover lying across the foot of one of the beds.

"Please be sure to attend your safety meeting station before the ship sails. It's mandatory for all new guests. Details of where to go are on the back of the door or on your TV. See you later," he said and left them to their unpacking.

"He's nice," said Donna, unlocking the suitcase on the bed. "Let's get unpacked, go and do this safety thing and then we're free to explore and find the best bar."

Twenty minutes later they had just about finished and, true to her word, Fiona had found a home for everything. If there was anything lacking it was coat hangers, but Fiona had already packed extra, so it didn't cause a problem. Another knock at the door caught her midway to the bathroom with an armful of cosmetics.

"Hello," said the smartly dressed young man. "I'm Nigel Williams, Entertainments Manager." Fiona took his outstretched hand. "Are you Fiona Campbell?"

"Yes, I am," Fiona replied, "and this is my friend, Donna Chambers. Please, come in."

"Just wanted to touch base with you and give you the itinerary for the talks on board," he said, walking past her and into the cabin and placing a few sheets of A4 paper on the dressing table. "You have a couple of days before you start. We'll catch up again nearer the time and I'll show you around the back of the theatre and introduce you to our techies. We have several more speakers on board, some will disembark in New York, and others will join us there. You'll meet some of the others at dinner this evening. We usually put those doing the whole trip together on the same table, but you can always ask the maître d' if you prefer to change."

"Thank you, Nigel, I'm sure we'll be just fine," said Fiona.

"Well, I'll leave you to it now. I'll see you around, but if you need me for anything, my number is on the list by the phone. I will leave any more bits and pieces I have for you in your postbox just outside your door. Don't forget the safety briefing."

"He seems alright," said Donna as the cabin door closed behind him.

"Yeah, but it doesn't really matter as long as he does his job. I doubt that I'll see that much of him."

"Right, lady, let's get this safety thing over and done with and then hit the bar."

Chapter II

Meeting their dinner companions that evening was interesting, to say the least. As a waiter led them through the dining room to their table towards the rear of the ship, Donna couldn't help but be impressed by the size and grandeur of the place. Every table looked elegant with pristine linens and perfectly aligned crockery and cutlery. She felt the buzz of energy as guests greeted one another and new friendships were being forged. From their table they had a wonderful view through tall panoramic windows. The sun had begun its journey towards the horizon and as it sunk lower shades of red, orange and pink lit up the sky and glinted off the water.

One couple had already claimed their places at their table and introduced themselves.

"Hello, I'm Alan and this is my wife, Sue. I'm a retired customs officer at Heathrow and fellow speaker."

"I'm a retired paediatric nurse," said Sue, "but not a speaker, thank heavens. Alan's the one that does all the talking, I just accompany him and enjoy the trip."

"Lovely to meet you both," said Fiona. "I'm Fiona and this is my friend, Donna. Are you getting off in New York or doing the Caribbean too?" asked Fiona.

"Oh, we're going all the way," laughed Alan. "I've got three talks on the way out and three on the way back, so roughly six hours' work in a couple of weeks is not bad, is it?"

"I'm the same," replied Fiona. "I'm a forensic psychologist and my boss asked if I would like to do the talks as he couldn't make it. It's a fabulous opportunity for Donna and me to spend some time in New York."

"What do you do, Donna?" asked Sue.

"I'm a nurse in charge of the Cardiac Unit at Hinchingbrooke Hospital in Huntingdon."

"We have a lot in common then," replied Sue.

Two women arrived, and introductions started again.

"Hello, everyone. I'm Carol and this is my daughter, Jessica."

"Hello, Carol and Jessica," said Alan. "What do you two ladies do?"

"We run a private investigations agency in Cardiff. I'm the one doing the talks on this trip."

"Do you take turns in speaking then?" asked Sue.

"Yes, sometimes we have done," Carol replied. "Although I must admit I think I enjoy it more than Jess does." Jessica nodded her head in agreement.

"Whatever inspired you to run an investigation agency?" asked Donna, intrigued.

"When I retired at fifty-five I felt I was too young to just do nothing, and as an ex-police detective it seemed a good fit."

"It was a ludicrous idea," laughed Jessica, "but surprisingly, it's doing really well.

Donna was intrigued by these two women and marvelled at Carol starting her own business after retirement.

"Wow, Fi, we could do that."

"Don't be daft, we don't have the experience," Fiona replied.

"We have some. We have Rhodes, Sardinia and Malaysia; if that's not experience, I don't know what is."

"Oh Donna, honestly," Fiona laughed. "Carol is an ex-detective and has years of experience. We have three holidays, and the police were involved each time."

"Now I'm curious," said Carol, "and I would love to know more."

"Maybe one evening we'll tell you over a drink," suggested Donna.

"I'll look forward to that," replied Carol. Jess nodded in agreement.

A man and two women were next to arrive and took their seats.

"I'm sorry we're late," said the man. "We were waiting for Eileen to find her medication, again. I do hope we haven't held you up."

"Not at all," said Alan. "We're all happily getting to know one another. I'm Alan and this is my wife, Sue."

"I'm Fiona and this is my friend, Donna."

"And I'm Carol and this is my daughter, Jess."

"A very good evening to you all. I'm William, my wife Eileen and my secretary Jenny. As you probably realise, I'm the lecturer. I'm a retired GP."

As the three were settling into their seats, William between his two ladies, another guest joined them and claimed the final place.

"Sorry to be last. I promise to do better tomorrow. Hello, everyone, I'm Winfield, but please call me Win. I gather we're on this table because we're some of the ship's speakers. I'm a wildlife photographer and I'll be talking about my many adventures trying to get the perfect shot."

"Wow," said Donna, "that sounds fascinating. I love animals and there's something magical about seeing them in the wild."

"Yes, there is," Win replied.

Two waiters hovered, ready to take their orders.

"Hello, everyone – welcome. I'm Frederic and this is JoJo, and we will be your waiters for the entire cruise. Any problems and we will do our very best to sort them out for you. The sommelier will be with you shortly to take your drinks orders, but in the meantime have you chosen what you would like to eat this evening?"

Frederic, from the Philippines, had a ready smile and a jovial personality. He regaled them with endless anecdotes throughout the evening, which they seriously doubted the authenticity of. JoJo, also from the Philippines, was the exact opposite. He was quieter but had a lovely smiling face that was endearing, especially to the ladies. The wine waiter brought their drinks and easy conversation flowed around the table. The food was delicious, although William managed to find something to complain about. Frederic was quick to change his plate and Fiona heard Eileen tell him to just eat it and stop moaning about everything. Lingering over coffee, it quickly became obvious that the staff were eager to get rid of them so they could prepare for the next sitting.

"Where are you off to now?" asked Alan, as the girls prepared to make a move.

"We thought we'd take in the show and then we'll more than likely end up somewhere where there's some good live music," replied Donna.

"We're off to one of the lounges for something quieter, but enjoy your evening."

"See you around, ladies," said Win. "Have fun!"

Chapter 12

"What do you think of our dinner companions?" asked Fiona, kicking off her strappy sandals as soon as they got back to their cabin. After the show, they had ended up in a lounge bar where a four-piece band played a variety of great music. The small dance floor was a bonus and the pair were on it most of the evening.

"Carol and Jess are interesting, and I look forward to getting to know them better. I really like Alan and Sue. They're a nice couple and he's quite amusing. Win is OK too and I look forward to hearing more about his work. The jury is still out on the other three."

"I agree with you. Really not sure about William; I thought he was a bit up himself."

"Agreed," said Donna. "He might be a big shot in his hometown, but here he's just an ordinary bloke. As my dear old aunt used to say, 'his shit still stinks'."

"Love that," Fiona laughed. "Loved your aunt too. She was such a character."

"Yeah, she was," Donna replied with a nostalgic smile on her face.

"William's wife Eileen seems quite sweet, but I'm not getting why he needed to bring Jenny with them. I mean, he's only doing a few talks, which he must have prepared before he left, so there can't be much for her to do."

"She's in love with him."

"Why do you say that?" asked Fiona.

"It's pretty obvious, really. Didn't you notice the way she looks at him?"

"No."

"You watch them tomorrow. Total adoration on her face."

"Do you think it's reciprocated?"

"Don't know," Donna replied. "He certainly didn't look at her in the same way, but then he had his wife sitting on the other side of him."

"One to watch, then?"

"Definitely," said Donna. "What do you think of Win?"

"A big gruff Scot with the heart of a pussycat. Seems nice enough."

"Is that all? I don't need to keep my eye on you then?"

"No, Donna, you don't," Fiona laughed. "Anyway, I couldn't do another romance at sea after Nikos." Fiona had a holiday romance with Nikos several years ago in Rhodes. He had agreed to them staying on his yacht to keep them safe from a drug smuggling gang. Their romance blossomed a little more when they spent another week together after the girls' Sardinian trip. Sadly, Nikos suffered a massive heart attack and died a year ago.

"You still miss him a lot, don't you?"

"Yes, I do," Fiona replied. "It's not a constant pain anymore, but now and then something will remind me of him and those feelings come flooding back. I loved him very much and was almost ready to make the move to Rhodes to be with him, you know."

"I know, darling," replied Donna. "There will never be another Nikos, but you will find love again, I'm sure of that."

"I hope so," said Fiona, "but I'm certainly not looking for it. And even if I was, it wouldn't be with Win. I'm just not attracted to him."

"That's OK then. Let's get some sleep. We've got another busy day tomorrow."

"What are we doing tomorrow, then?" Fiona asked.

"Don't know, and that's half the fun."

Chapter 13

Leaving their cabin for their first full day at sea they headed up to the buffet restaurant.

"My God," said Donna, looking at the throng of people crowding into the space in front of the self-service area. "This ship is in danger of running out of supplies the way that lot are going at it."

"Let's try the main dining room," laughed Fiona. "I know it has waiter service so I'm sure it will be a bit more civilised."

They made their way back down to the main dining room and joined a short queue.

"Good morning, ladies," said a very smart young man as they reached the front desk. "Would you like to join a larger table, or is it just for two?"

"Can we have a table for two, please?" asked Fiona.

"Certainly. Your stateroom number, please?"

Fiona watched as he entered their number into the computer and beckoned to the next waiter.

"Joseph will escort you to your seats. Enjoy your breakfast, ladies."

"Oh lovely view," said Donna, as they took their seats by a window. "Such a beautiful day and the sea looks so tranquil."

"Let's hope it stays that way," laughed Fiona.

They had six days at sea before they reached New York and they hoped the crossing would be calm as they headed west. As they left Southampton the weather was fairly good, but who knew what raging turmoil the Atlantic Ocean might throw at them. There was a slight chill in the air which made it a bit too cool to sit out on deck without a jumper, but they hoped there would be plenty of time to soak up the sun as the days went on.

Fiona pulled the daily programme from her bag. It was waiting for them in their cabin the previous evening, and was crammed with things to do, classes to attend, speakers to listen to and shows to watch. The pair were determined to make the most of all the ship had to offer.

"Blimey," Donna exclaimed, "there's so much to do."

"What do you fancy?" asked Fiona.

"Alan's giving his first talk this morning, so might be worth going to that. I think it's probably too cold to be out on deck."

"OK, let's do that. Look, they do yoga in the mornings, it's a bit early but I might try and squeeze it in before breakfast."

"I'll come with you, providing I've not got a hangover," Donna laughed.

"Remember, we'll have a bar bill at the end of this trip. It's not like our usual all-inclusive Mediterranean holiday."

"True. There's a music quiz this afternoon. We'll be good at that."

"Bloody hell, Donna, you were right, it will be a busy day."

Finishing breakfast, they made their way to the other end of the ship for Alan's talk. The theatre was filling up fast, but as they walked down the steps, they found a couple of seats near to the front. Alan was an excellent speaker and kept the attention of his audience with lots of humorous anecdotes of the many items and inventive ways passengers used to smuggle goods into the country.

"I enjoyed that very much," said Fiona as they left the theatre. "I only hope I keep my audience's attention as well as he did."

"I'm sure you will, babe, just keep the humour flowing. Oh look, there's Eileen."

"She looks a bit lost," said Fiona as the girls made their way over to her.

"Hello, Eileen," said Fiona, "where are you off to?"

"I'm not sure," she replied. "I need to find my medication, it keeps going missing. It's my heart you see, I need to take digoxin to keep it ticking."

"Are you heading back to your cabin?" asked Donna.

"I suppose I am, but I'm not sure which way to go."

"What deck are you on? Do you know your cabin number?" asked Fiona.

"No, I can't remember." Eileen was getting agitated.

"Where's William?" asked Donna.

"He's gone off with Jenny, he said they had work to do." Donna shot Fiona a look over Eileen's head.

"Don't worry, we'll get you back to your cabin," said Donna, "but first we need to go down to the main desk to find out the number."

"What a coincidence," said Fiona as she noted the cabin number, "you're along the same corridor as us."

Thirty minutes later, they saw Eileen safely back into her cabin. The girls followed her in, just to make sure she was settled.

"There they are," Eileen exclaimed, looking puzzled. "They weren't there earlier when I looked, I'm sure of it."

"Perhaps they had fallen on the floor and your steward picked them up," suggested Fiona.

"Maybe," Eileen replied. "I need these, you see. They're for my heart, so I need to take them regularly."

"Well, you have them now, so all is well. Why don't you have a little rest?" suggested Donna.

"Yes, I think I will."

Chapter 14

Fiona had a meeting with Nigel later that afternoon, in readiness for her first talk the following day. She had given several talks in the past, but they were mainly to students, this time she could feel the nerves building. In theory, this lecture should be easy, as her audience would probably not have a clue what she was talking about, but there was always the chance there might be one expert among them.

Nigel was a nice enough guy, in a very clean, scrubbed in antiseptic, kind of way. Donna had said he was pink and would have put him as an accountant rather than an entertainments manager. He reminded her of a man she used to work with in an accountant's office during her school holidays. He sat alone in his office all day with the door shut and whenever she went in, there was a furtive rustling in his desk drawer and a strong smell of antiseptic hung in the air. A few years later, an article in their local newspaper reported that he had been found guilty of stealing ladies' underwear from washing lines.

Nigel loved his job, even though a slight air of panic seemed to be his permanent companion. He wished he could stop thinking of all the things that could go wrong and concentrate on what went right. Nigel had been in the entertainment business since he graduated from Northampton University with a degree in events management.

"Hello, Fiona, how are you this afternoon?" he asked, as Fiona joined him at the front of the theatre.

"I'm fine, thanks, Nigel. How are you?"

"Yes all good with me. I'm looking forward to a quieter few days at sea now that all the speakers and entertainers are on board. It's just a matter of getting everyone to the right place at the right time and making sure our guests are enjoying themselves."

"Don't you ever get fed up with life at sea?" she asked.

"I hope I won't. This is my first cruise ship so at the moment it's still a bit of a novelty. Previously, I've been in holiday camps and hotels."

"Not sure I would like to be away from my family and friends for so long."

"It works well if you're young, free and single. You soon find your circle of friends among the staff. They become your new family."

"I guess so." Fiona was unconvinced.

"Right, Fiona, let me show you how this all works and then you'll be all set for tomorrow."

Chapter 15

Much later, as they left the cocktail bar after their pre-dinner drinks, they bumped into William heading towards the dining room.

"Hello, William," said Donna, "on your own tonight?"

"No, no. Eileen and Jenny have gone on ahead. I forgot something, so had to go back to the cabin."

"We bumped into Eileen earlier," said Fiona. "She seemed a little confused and couldn't remember your cabin number."

"She was looking for her medication," Donna continued. "She was rather anxious about it. We eventually got the cabin number and took her back. Funnily enough, we seem to be neighbours as well as dinner companions as your cabin is just a few along from us. Anyway, her tablets were on the dressing table so she calmed down and said she would have a little rest. I hope she's feeling better now."

"Yes, she's OK now. Between us, I'm convinced she is suffering from the beginnings of dementia. She gets so stressed, particularly over her tablets, and is forever misplacing them, or so she says."

"What does she take the tablets for?" asked Fiona.

"Her heart. She's convinced that without them she will die."

"And will she?" asked Fiona.

"No, of course not. It's all in her head." As they reached the dining room, William changed the conversation. "Ah, everyone is already here." William took his place between Eileen and Jenny, which prevented either of the girls from quizzing him further.

"Evening, everyone," said Donna, taking her seat.

"How did your first talk go this morning, Alan?" asked Fiona.

"I think it went well," he replied.

"You know it went well, Fi, we were there," Donna laughed.

"Yes," replied Fiona, "but there's a big difference between how the audience felt it went and how you feel it went."

"That's true," said Alan. "The audience seemed to enjoy it, laughed in all the right places and asked lots of questions at the end. From my point of view, it was as good as it could be, and there were no glitches with the slides. Although I always prepare, what I really like to do is simply talk to the audience rather than read notes. I feel I'm talking to them rather than at them."

"That's interesting," said Fiona, "because the best part for me are the questions at the end. I feel I'm answering from the heart rather than a rehearsed set piece. Well, I hope I'm half as good as you in the morning."

Dinner was once again delicious, although William managed to find something that didn't quite suit. Both girls enjoyed their choices, plus the bottle of wine they shared. The group around the table chatted amicably, except for Jenny who really didn't say much at all.

"Right," said Donna, after they had finished their coffee, "we're off to the show. Enjoy your evening and we'll see you all tomorrow."

As they meandered down towards the theatre, Carol and Jess caught up with them.

"We're off to the show too," said Carol, "and I'm wondering if you two fancy joining us for a few drinks in the Gin Bar after? We can spend some time getting to know each other and you can tell us all about these holidays of yours."

"Sounds good to me," said Donna. "Fiona, OK with you?"

"Oh yes, perfect," Fiona replied.

"Great," replied Carol. "Whoever gets there first, grab four seats."

The show was good, a comedian who had his audience in fits of laughter from beginning to end and the girls were still laughing as they left the theatre.

"I loved that, Fi," said Donna. "It's so good to laugh."

"Yes, it is and he was fantastic, just what we needed to kick off the holiday. Now, which way to the Gin Bar?"

Donna pulled out a little booklet from her bag, which opened to show deck plans of the ship.

"This way," she said, and took off towards the grand staircase.

Carol and Jess had already claimed a table by the time the girls arrived. Donna had got them lost three times before finally stopping and asking for directions. Jess stood and waved as soon as she spotted them coming through the doors.

"I thought not asking for directions was just a man thing, but you've just wasted half an hour," laughed Fiona. Donna said nothing.

"Sorry we're late," said Fiona, as she weaved her way through the tables. "I have no idea how anyone can get as lost as we did on a cruise ship when they have a map in front of them. We nearly ended up in the kitchens."

"Oh believe me, it's an easy thing to do," laughed Carol, signalling to a nearby waiter. "It's only because we've been on this ship a couple of times before that we've sussed out where everything is."

"Do you do this speaking thing often then?" asked Donna, once the waiter had taken their orders.

"Yes, once or twice a year. It's a doddle really, and it gets us a holiday."

"But don't you have to keep rewriting the talks?" asked Fiona.

"Yes and no. Remember, these people are only on board for a couple of weeks and the likelihood of seeing them again is pretty slim, so you can use the same talk quite a few times. Now and then, I update them on the new stuff that's happened. It works really well for me."

"There you are," Donna looked at Fiona. "You can get yourself more bookings on ships and we can cruise the seven seas."

The four women spent the next few hours sharing stories, drinking gin and laughing a lot.

Chapter 16

Fiona's first talk of the trip went well. She was pleased with the turnout and delighted with the number of questions asked at the end. Although forensic psychology was a serious subject, she kept it light, humorous and entertaining, and had her audience captivated.

Donna was really impressed. She had never heard Fi speak before and was amazed at how accomplished her friend was.

Fiona felt she could relax a little now and take the rest of her lectures more or less in her stride. In a show of solidarity for their fellow dinner companions, the girls checked out all the other talks. Most were interesting, but that was mainly because of the delivery of the speaker. Sadly, William's talks left a lot to be desired. He took every opportunity to remind his audience of his importance, what a popular man he was and how they should all feel totally reassured and grateful that he was on board.

The girls stole out the back of the theatre one afternoon, unable to sit through more tedious diatribe and self-inflating remarks from William. They headed towards the top deck and claimed a couple of sunbeds around the small pool. The weather was glorious, with a clear blue sky and just enough breeze to keep them cool. Music streamed from the speakers, loud enough to hear but not too loud to hinder conversation.

"Honestly," said Fiona. "That man is far too sure of himself. He was a GP for God's sake, not a world class brain surgeon. I'm not saying that GPs are insignificant, but they are just normal people doing their job."

"I agree," replied Donna. "You know, I can remember my aunt calling her doctor 'sir', like he was some kind of god. Used to drive me up the wall. I'm all for respect, but I think that's taking it to the limit. People like William do my head in. To be honest, Fi, I have a strange feeling about him."

"In what way?" asked Fiona.

"Not sure, but all is not what it seems. This business with Eileen doesn't feel right either."

"Is this one of your 'feelings'?" asked Fiona, making air quotes.

"Possibly. Would be good to see what Carol and Jess think of the threesome."

"Let's invite them for a drink later."

"We can, but don't let's spend every night with them or we won't get the chance to sing and dance."

Fiona laughed. There was nothing Donna liked more than getting on the dance floor and strutting her stuff. Add in some singing and Donna was in heaven.

"You should have been on the stage, Don."

"I should, shouldn't I?" The girls laughed.

"Hello, you two, having fun?"

"Oh hello, Jess," said Fiona. "We were just agreeing that Donna should be on the stage, given how she loves to sing and dance. But then you haven't seen that side of her yet."

"Well maybe I should," replied Jessica. "I love nothing better than a good night out, maybe Mum and I could join you one night?"

"Of course you can," said Donna. "Talking of your mum, what's she up to?"

"Checking her emails," Jess replied, clearly not happy. "I thought this would be the ideal way to spend some time together, after she's done the talks of course, but work always comes first. The first thing she did when we got on board was sign up for Wi-Fi."

"But you work together," said Fiona, "so you must spend time with each other every day."

"We see each other of course, but it's all about the work and not quality mother and daughter time. I miss that."

"Have you told her how you feel?" asked Donna.

"No, what would be the point?"

"Because unless you tell her how you feel, you can't really expect her to understand how much you miss her and how it affects you."

"I suppose you're right," Jessica said grudgingly.

"There must be times when the two of you are alone. Why not suggest you go for a walk around the deck or a drink and then talk? You probably don't have the time or get the chance at home, so make the most of being here and talk to her from the heart."

"Thank you, Donna. You know, I'm going to do that today. See you both later."

"Blimey, Don, for someone so very down to earth, you can be so very wise at times," said Fiona, smiling at her best friend.

"Do you know, Fi, sometimes words come pouring out of my mouth and I have no idea where they come from."

Fiona laughed, reached across the sunbed and picked up her friend's hand.

"I love you, Donna Chambers. Don't ever change, will you?"

Chapter 17

Why on earth did I ever agree to come on this trip? Eileen wondered as she paced backwards and forwards around the cabin.

I thought it would be a good way to spend some quality time with William, away from the pressures of home and those people who demand his attention. But he had to bring her along, didn't he, and now he's spending most of his time with her. Why does she have to be here? Surely he can manage to give a couple of talks without needing his secretary. Why does he still need her anyway? They're both retired from the surgery.

I wish I felt a bit better. I don't like this fluttering in my chest, but maybe it's to be expected with my condition. I feel a bit sick too, probably a bit of seasickness. It will pass. I'll check it out with William when he deigns to come back.

I know I must treat my heart condition seriously and take my medication regularly. I do listen to what he tells me, but how can I take the pills when they keep disappearing? He told me it was my fault that I keep mislaying them, because I never put them away properly. But I always put them in the same place, the top drawer by my bed.

He told me the other morning that I was losing the plot. He got quite cross with me. It was the morning those two nice women brought me back to the cabin. What were their names? Donna and Fiona, that was it. They are lovely and very kind to me. They found the pill bottle on the dressing table, but I know it wasn't there when

I looked. They thought the steward might have picked them up when he came in to clean the room. I suppose that's possible.

I hope I'm not getting dementia.

Oh William, where are you? With Jenny I expect. But I could do with you here with me. I want you to reassure me that I'm not getting dementia, and that my heart won't give out anytime soon.

I think I'll have a little nap before dinner, then maybe I will feel better.

Oh William, please come and put my mind at rest.

Chapter 18

Jenny snuggled closer into the warmth of William's body. Although it wasn't cold in the cabin, she could feel cool air blowing across her naked body from the air conditioning unit high on the wall. The pair were lying on top of Jenny's king-size bed, happy and content after their vigorous lovemaking session.

"I suppose I'd better go and check on Eileen," muttered William.

"Oh don't go yet, I'm sure she'll be fine. Let's just have five more minutes."

Jenny wondered if there would ever come a day when she would have William all to herself, to go to sleep with him and wake up with him still lying next to her. She hated having to share him with Eileen, but it was better than not having him at all, she reasoned.

Jenny idolised William. From the very first day she joined the local doctors' surgery as the secretary, she felt an attraction that she couldn't explain. She swelled with pride when William told her he felt he could totally rely on her to keep the practice running smoothly. Over the years, her attraction to him grew stronger until finally the pair ended up in bed together after a few too many drinks at the staff Christmas party.

She wasn't happy they were deceiving Eileen, but she loved William with all her heart and if that was the price she had to pay to get her man, then so be it. He had told her many times that he would never leave his wife. He was far too status conscious and worried what the community might think if he were to run off with his secretary.

Jenny sighed as she felt him move away from her, their time together over.

***

William knew he needed to check on Eileen. Earlier that morning she had complained of feeling unwell, heart palpitations and nausea. But Jenny's body was warm and comforting and when she suggested another five minutes, he readily agreed.

William wasn't in love with Jenny, not in the way she wanted him to be. But he liked her well enough, she was available and it suited his needs to have her with him.

Eileen had become quite distant since they diagnosed her heart condition. Obsessed with her health, all she had time for was herself. God, the woman never shut up. She talked all day about how she felt, what was wrong with her, should she be doing this, that or the other. William had just about had enough and Jenny was a useful distraction. She scratched an itch.

But he wanted his life to change.

Since his son had taken over the practice, he had begun to feel a level of freedom that he had never previously experienced. Options were opening up to him, but he kept them to himself. He didn't want to worry Eileen, and he certainly didn't want Jenny getting any inkling of what he was considering.

This cruise had given him the perfect opportunity to make some life changes.

Chapter 19

"I'm so glad that Matt and Jason decided to rent Tom's house, aren't you?" Donna asked, as she settled down on her sunbed. The weather had improved substantially since leaving the UK and although the girls were finding more than enough to do inside the ship, a couple of hours in the sun never went amiss.

"Oh yes, I agree," replied Fiona. "It's so lovely to have them with us, but it will be sad when Tom comes home and wants his house back."

"Yeah, that will be bittersweet, but a lot can happen between now and then. What do you think of Jason's brother?"

"I liked him, but then he's a lot like Jason and there's nothing to dislike there. What about you?"

"Yeah, I liked him too, although we didn't really see that much of him. I guess he will be around a lot more now the boys have moved in."

"Mmm, expect so."

"What shall we do this evening?" asked Donna.

"I wouldn't mind going to the ballroom. They've got that band who were in the theatre the other night, so there'll be great music to dance to."

"And sing to," laughed Donna, as Fiona rolled her eyes upwards.

"I think we should do the show first though, then we'll miss the sequence dancing."

"Agreed," Donna replied. "Perhaps Carol and Jess would like to join us, they look like they're up for a good time too."

"We'll ask them at dinner. I think, sugar, it's now time we went back to the cabin and got ready for this evening, especially if you want a cocktail before dinner."

As they made their way back, they bumped into William coming out of one of the cabins along their corridor.

"Hi William, how's things?" asked Donna.

"Oh hello, ladies, yes, all is fine thank you."

"Is Eileen OK today?" asked Fiona.

"She's as well as she can be," he replied. "Now, if you'll excuse me, I must go and check on her."

William let himself into the cabin next door to the one he had just left.

"That cabin he's just come out of is not the one we took Eileen back to the other day," said Donna.

"No, but the one he's just gone into is," replied Fiona.

"So what's he been doing in the first cabin, I wonder?"

"Jenny?"

The girls burst into fits of giggles and carried on down the corridor to their own cabin.

"You know, there's something about that man that I'm just not easy with. Can't quite put my finger on it, but I wouldn't trust him as far as I could throw him," said Donna, dumping her bag on the bed.

"We'll just have to keep an eye on him, then. Are you going in the bathroom first, or shall I?"

"You go, I'm just going to have ten minutes on the balcony."

Chapter 20

William quietly let himself into the cabin and found Eileen lying on her bed.

"Eileen," he called softly.

"Mmm," she murmured.

"How are you feeling?" he asked, as he perched on the edge and took her hand.

"I feel awful, William, my heart is racing and I feel so sick."

"It's just seasickness. I'll go and get you some tablets from the Infirmary and you'll feel as right as rain in a few hours."

"I hope so," she replied.

"It's probably best you stay here and rest this evening. You won't feel much like eating anyway."

"Will you stay with me?" Eileen asked, desperate not to be left alone.

"I would like to, my love, but it wouldn't be fair to leave Jenny on her own would it?"

"William, I'm your wife," Eileen replied, with as much annoyance as she could muster.

"I know, and believe me I would much rather be here by your side. But Jenny is doing so much for me on this cruise that I just don't think I should leave her on her own."

"She won't be on her own. She knows everyone at dinner and maybe Win would like to take her somewhere."

"I don't think that's likely," William snapped. "Look, I'm going to nip to the Infirmary and pick up some tablets for you. I won't be long."

William ran a hand down his face as he let the cabin door slam shut behind him. *Bloody woman*, he thought, *why did she have to be so bloody needy?*

Thirty minutes later he was back in his cabin. Eileen was still lying in the same position as when he left her.

"Oh William, I think I'm dying."

"Oh for heaven's sake, Eileen, you're suffering from a bout of seasickness which I know can make you feel pretty awful, but it will not kill you. Now take these, get some sleep and you'll feel much better in the morning."

He shook two tablets into his hand, poured a glass of water and handed them to his wife.

"Are you sure you won't stay with me?" she asked, slumping back down on the pillows.

"Darling, you will be asleep in no time so it would be pointless me sitting here watching you sleep. Besides, I still need to eat."

William quickly showered and changed and quietly let himself out of the cabin. Eileen was already asleep, the pills he had given her clearly doing their job.

"Ready?" he asked, as Jenny opened the door to his knock.

"Yes," she replied, stepping into the corridor. "Where's Eileen?"

"Sleeping. She's suffering from a bit of seasickness so best she rests. It's just you and me this evening."

"Perfect," she replied, taking his arm and gazing at him adoringly.

Chapter 21

"Sorry we're late," said Fiona, as the pair hurriedly took their places at the dinner table. Everyone had swapped seats so they could get to know all their companions a little better. That evening Fiona found herself between Win and Alan, whilst Donna had William one side and Carol the other.

"No Eileen tonight?" she asked as the waiter unfolded the napkin and draped it across her lap.

"No," said William. "Sadly she's suffering from a bit of seasickness so I've got her some medication from the Infirmary and it's best she sleeps it off."

"Probably is," agreed Donna. "I hope she feels better in the morning, such a shame to feel rough on holiday and miss this wonderful cruise."

"Indeed."

"I know you're a retired GP from Berkshire, William, but I know little about Eileen. What does she do? Or what did she do before retirement?"

"Eileen never really did much. It wasn't long after we married that she became pregnant with our first child, so she gave up her job in admin and became a full-time wife and mother. Our daughter was born a couple of years later and Eileen was perfectly happy with her lot in life."

"Didn't she ever want to do something for herself? I mean, I have three kids and I love them all to pieces, but sometimes I just wanted to be away from them and do something for myself."

"Oh no, Eileen was never like that. She has been a good wife in many respects. Always had dinner on the table when I came home, kept a clean and comfortable home, kept the children quiet when I wanted peace, and always waited up to make me a hot drink when I got a call out in the night."

"You say 'has been a good wife' as if she no longer is," laughed Donna.

"Did I? Well of course that's not what I mean, but things have changed over the years. Now I've retired, I don't need quite so much looking after, shall we say? Plus, I'm out of the house quite a lot."

"What do you do now you've retired?" Donna asked.

"Oh I play a bit of golf, meet up with old pals. I do give lectures from time to time, and of course there are the cruises, so they all need to be written and admin work done."

"Presumably Jenny helps with those?"

"Yes, she does. She's a great help."

I bet she is, thought Donna as she felt Carol's hand on her arm, claiming her attention.

"What are you doing this evening?" Carol asked.

"We're off to the ballroom. Apparently that really good Motown band who were on stage the other night are playing in there, so there'll be a good dancing opportunity. Do you want to join us?"

"Love to," said Jess, leaning in front of her mother before she could say anything.

"Fabulous," replied Donna. "We're going to the show first so we don't get caught up in the sequence dancing, but as soon as we're out of the theatre we'll hotfoot it down and grab a table."

"Perfect," replied Carol. "We'll do the same but I will probably send Jess on ahead because she can run faster in heels."

"Oh I know the feeling," laughed Donna, "but I'm not quite ready to give up fashion for comfort yet. Mind you, I feel that time is quickly approaching, and these will be kicked off five minutes after getting in the ballroom."

They chatted and laughed their way through the rest of dinner. Alan and Sue were good company, Win regaled them with many stories of his attempts to get the best wildlife photo, William was happy talking about himself. Only Jenny was quiet; she spoke when she was spoken to but never contributed to the conversation. Donna had to wonder why.

Chapter 22

Fiona kicked off her sandals after just ten minutes. Her feet were already killing her and it was shaping up to be a long night. She hoped the other dancers would steer clear of her personal space and not grind her toes into the floor. The four of them danced, sang and drank far more than they intended to, and Donna was definitely a strong contender for 'dancer of the cruise' award. Sadly, the same couldn't be said for 'singer of the cruise'. When the band took a break, so did the girls.

"What do you think of William and his two women?" asked Carol.

"All is not what it seems," Donna replied.

"How do you mean?"

"Hard to put it into words," Donna said.

"For as long as I've known her, Donna has always had these feelings," Fiona broke in. "I didn't think too much of it when we were younger, but recently they have become much stronger and, I have to say, she's usually right."

"So what are these feelings telling you about William?" asked Jess.

"That he's not to be trusted."

"What I don't understand," said Carol, "is why he had to bring his secretary with him. Surely he would have prepared his talks before he left."

"Exactly what I said, Carol," Fiona said. "I mean, what does she do all day?"

"When we went back to the cabin earlier, William was coming out of the room next to theirs, which we guessed would be Jenny's," added Donna.

"Then that's what she does all day," laughed Jess.

"What do you mean?" asked her mother.

"Oh come on, Mum, it doesn't take much to work out that William is having his cake and eating it, or rather his secretary."

"Do you really think so?" asked Carol.

"Yes!" the three women exclaimed together.

"Think about it, Carol," said Fiona. "Why has he brought Jenny with him? Jenny absolutely adores the man and Eileen is unwell and hardly the life and soul of the holiday. My guess is this was too good an opportunity for William and Jenny to spend most of their time together, leaving poor old Eileen on her own."

"And they would only have to pay for one ticket," added Donna.

"Well if that's all it is, then good luck to the pair of them. But I do feel sorry for Eileen."

"I don't think that's all it is," said Donna. "There's more going on there, and I intend to find out what it is."

"Do you think he's drugging Eileen to keep her quiet so he can spend more time with Jenny?" asked Jess.

"It's possible," Donna replied, "but I think there's a lot more than that."

"Donna," warned Fiona. "Don't turn this trip into another of our innocents abroad capers."

"No, babe, I won't. But if I keep getting these feelings then you know I have to do something about it."

"Can't you talk to Angelo?" asked Fiona.

"You know it's not that easy."

"Who's Angelo?" asked Jess.

"That, my love, is a story for another time," replied Donna watching the band make their way back on stage and pick up their instruments for another set.

With the opening chords of Cyndi Lauper's 'Girls Just Want to Have Fun' springing to life, Donna's and Fiona's heads immediately whipped round as they looked at each other. A smile, a high five and the pair skipped their way to the dance floor, clapping and singing as they went.

"They're playing our song," Fi said to Carol as she passed.

Chapter 23

With just two more days at sea before they hit New York, Donna and Fiona spent their time between some morning exercise, a few quizzes, lying in the sun, supporting their fellow speakers and eating. Life at sea was bliss, and Donna could certainly see how people became addicted to cruising. So much to do during the day, so much variety for nightlife, the food was plentiful and fabulous, plus lots of new places to visit when the ship docked. She wondered if Dave might fancy it.

She was enjoying the freedom of not having to check in with him every day. She missed him, of course, but since her previous holidays with Fiona had led to some scary moments, Dave insisted she check in with him daily. This trip, however, limited her opportunities to do that. Not much harm could come to them on a cruise ship and anyway, the internet charges were steep and she refused to pay them. He would just have to wait until they reached New York and she could connect to some free Wi-Fi.

"Shall we get something to eat?" she asked, looking at her watch. Fiona had just emerged from a cooling dip in the pool and flopped down on her sunbed.

"OK, but give me ten minutes to dry off a bit and then we'll go in."

Fifteen minutes later they made their way to the self-service restaurant and bumped into William and Jenny just leaving.

"Hello, you two," said Fiona. "Eileen still unwell?"

"Yes, I'm afraid so. Still in bed when I left this morning, but I'm just on my way back to check on her now and to make sure she takes her lunchtime medication."

"I hope you find her a bit brighter. Give her our best wishes for a speedy recovery," said Donna.

"Will do," replied William, his hand in the small of Jenny's back as he guided her towards the lifts.

"For a man whose wife has spent the first few days of their holiday ill in bed, he doesn't seem too upset, does he?" said Fiona.

"No, certainly doesn't," replied Donna. "I hope he does check on her and not head off for some afternoon delight with Jenny."

"Mmm, hope so too."

"I have to wonder," said Donna, as they grabbed a table by the full-length window that a couple had just vacated, "what does he see in Jenny? She's not exactly arm candy or lively, is she?"

"That's probably why he's with her," replied Fiona, signalling for the drinks waiter. "She allows him to shine."

They ordered a couple of beers and tucked into their lunch. Fiona had chosen a sensible salad whilst Donna added lots of coleslaw to her plate and a generous slice of pizza.

"I'm worried about Eileen," said Donna.

"In what way?" asked Fiona.

"I don't know, but this just doesn't feel right. I find it odd that he's brought his secretary on holiday with them, and it's a bit too convenient for his wife to get sick and leave the pair of them alone, don't you think?"

"Yes, but people do get sick on cruise ships, so it might be coincidence."

"I'd really like to go and check on Eileen myself," Donna exclaimed.

"Not sure that's a good idea, Don."

"It's an excellent idea. Come on." Donna pushed her plate away and stood up to leave.

"Donna!" warned Fiona.

"I'm going to check. You can either come or not, up to you, sugar."

"Well then, I'll have to come because you're not going on your own."

Donna knocked on William's door. She could hear movement inside and hoped that meant Eileen was out of bed and feeling better. The door opened a crack.

"Oh, it's you," said William, just a thin slice of his face showing.

"Sorry, William, but we just wanted to see how Eileen was doing. We're worried about her."

"She's sleeping," he said, stepping back to close the door. Donna took the opportunity and pushed it open a little further. Fiona caught a glimpse of Jenny standing over the bed looking down at Eileen, her hands over her mouth and her face as white as a sheet.

"What's happened, William?" Fiona asked in a serious tone.

"Um, I've no idea, but Eileen is not responding." He tried to close the door again.

"What do you mean you have no idea? You're a bloody doctor for God's sake." Donna put all her weight against the door and pushed it fully open, walked into the cabin and over to Eileen's bed.

"Oh my God, Fi, she's dead."

Chapter 24

"Have you called this in, William?" asked Donna, after checking Eileen for a pulse, her nursing training coming to the fore. She looked up at Fiona and gave an imperceptible shake of the head at her friend's raised eyebrows.

"No, not yet. We've only just got back. Now I think you two need to leave and let us deal with this."

"William, you must be in shock," soothed Fiona. "Why don't you both sit down and let us call the medical centre for you? It's the least we can do."

"No, I can deal with this thank you. Out you go."

Donna wasn't listening and moved towards the phone as Fiona guided William and Jenny to the two chairs around the low coffee table. Jenny looked totally shocked, her skin as white as a ghost and wide eyes, like a rabbit caught in headlights. William was expressionless.

Donna briefly and succinctly explained the situation to the medics and within minutes there was a knock on the cabin door.

Fiona let the medical officer and a nurse into the cabin.

"Thank you, ladies, but I think we can manage now so you can both get on with your day," said William in a very authoritative manner, moving to escort them out.

"I'm sorry, sir, but we need everybody to remain until we can discover what has happened here," said the medical officer, preparing to examine Eileen. Pulling on a pair of blue surgical gloves, he checked the carotid artery in her neck for a pulse and after several seconds, slightly shook his head as he made eye contact with the nurse.

"Is she dead?" asked William.

"I'm very sorry, sir, but I'm afraid she is."

Moving away from the bed the nurse pulled her pager from the pocket of her trousers.

"Operation Rising Star," they heard her say, followed by the cabin number.

"Can you tell me a little about your wife's medical history, sir?" asked the medical officer.

"Yes, well, she had a history of heart problems so I'm presuming this is a heart attack?"

"We can't be sure of that at this stage, but it's a high probability. Any other conditions?"

"No," said William. "I was her GP so I knew her medical history."

"But surely she was registered with a different GP or practice?"

"It's not illegal to treat one's own family," bristled William.

"No it isn't," replied the officer, "but it's highly unethical and the General Medical Council warns against it."

"Yes, well, that's easier said than done when you live in a small town with just a one-man practice. She was always mislaying her medication, and misjudging the dose. I warned her time after time of the dangers of missing a dose."

"I'm very sorry for your loss, sir. Our team will be here shortly and they will guide you as to what happens next, which should be fairly straightforward. Can I just check what medication she was taking please?"

William readily gave the information, including the dosage of each pill. The medic appeared satisfied as he jotted details down in his notepad. The knock on the cabin door heralded the arrival of the team, including the security officer.

"Ahh," said the medic, "here's our Care Team and Susannah here will help and guide you through the next stages. I have to leave now, but if you have any questions for me, please let Susannah know. Once again, I am very sorry for your loss."

"Hello, William," said Susannah, taking over from the medic. "I'm your first point of contact as to what happens next, so as Mike has already said, if you have any questions or need any help at all, just contact me." She handed William a piece of paper with her name and contact number on.

"So the first thing we have to do is take Eileen down to the Infirmary. She will rest there until we arrive in New York, where she will disembark and the formalities completed in preparation for repatriation. You will disembark with her and arrangements for your return home will be made for you."

"What if I want to stay on board?" asked William.

"That's unusual, but of course it's your choice. Arrangements will still be made for your wife."

"Jenny, my secretary, and I will stay on board and return to the UK as scheduled."

"Fine," said Susannah. "We will need to take more details from you, but that can come later. I suggest we move to a vacant cabin so the team can help Eileen."

"Bit late to help Eileen now, isn't it?" William snapped.

"We will treat Eileen with the utmost care and respect, Dr Mitchell, but there are protocols that we have to follow. Pete, our Security Officer, will need to ask a few questions." Susannah moved towards the door.

"Why do we need the security officer?" asked William. "We already know that Eileen died of a heart attack, so what exactly do you hope to achieve here?"

"I'm sorry, sir, but it's standard procedure," said Pete. "First of all, we don't know for certain what caused Eileen's death; that still needs to be confirmed. I just need to go over a few questions with you all, so I can write and submit my report to the authorities in New York."

Susannah led them to an unoccupied cabin on the same deck, where they spent the next half an hour or so answering Pete's questions. Finally, the girls left the cabin, leaving William and Jenny alone with the team.

Chapter 25

"Wow, didn't see that one coming," said Fiona when they were back in their own cabin.

"Oh I did," said Donna, moving to the desk and picking up the phone.

"Who are you phoning?" asked Fiona, still perplexed by the whole afternoon.

"Carol and Jess. They need to hear about this before we go to dinner."

"True," said Fiona. "Wonder if William and Jenny will join us this evening."

"Yeah, I wonder. Bugger, they're not answering. I'll leave a message – 'Carol, Jess, we have developments. Gin Bar at five o'clock. Will fill you in then' – let's hope they hear that before dinner tonight."

"They'll probably head back to the cabin soon to get ready for dinner, so will pick it up then," said Fiona. "Shall I go into the bathroom first? For some reason it seems to take me longer to get ready."

"That's because you faff about so much with your appearance. I could understand it if you were ugly, but you're not so it should take you half the time."

"It's because all the hairs sprouting out of my chin are taking longer and longer to pluck out!"

"Know the feeling, babe, and it only gets worse," Donna laughed.

"My fear is that I'll end up looking like a female version of Brian Blessed."

Thirty minutes later they left the cabin and headed off to the Gin Bar. There was no sign of Carol or Jess when they arrived. Grabbing a table, Donna ordered four large gin and tonics.

"Blimey, Don, what happens if they don't come?"

"Then we'll have to drink them, which would be a great shame," laughed Donna.

Twenty minutes later Carol and Jess rushed in.

"So sorry," said Carol. "We didn't see the phone blinking until gone five."

"It's fine. Here," said Fiona, pushing their drinks across the table. "We got a gin and tonic for you both."

"Wonderful, thanks," said Carol, taking a large gulp from her glass.

"You will not believe this," Donna began. "Eileen's dead."

"What?" squealed Jess as Carol choked on a mouthful of gin.

"Yes, afraid so," said Fiona. "We bumped into William and Jenny on the Lido Deck at lunch time. He said Eileen was still unwell and had stayed in bed all morning. He was heading back to check on her."

"I felt uneasy about the whole thing," said Donna, "so after we had eaten we went down to their cabin to check for ourselves."

"He didn't want to let us in," added Fiona, "but I glimpsed Jenny standing over the bed with her head in her hands."

"Bloody hell," gasped Carol.

"I knew something wasn't quite right," continued Donna, "so I pushed the door and we went in and found Eileen dead."

"Where's Eileen now?" asked Jess.

"In the Infirmary," Fiona replied. "She'll be taken off the ship in New York. The authorities there will deal with everything before issuing a death certificate and then she'll be flown back home."

"Would you believe that William and Jenny will stay on board for the rest of the trip and he'll deal with everything when they get home?"

"That doesn't really surprise me," said Carol. "That man seems so full of himself that a little thing like his wife's death will not stop him getting what he wants. What's the betting he'll use the excuse of being a speaker and not wanting to let his audience down?"

"There is one more thing before we go off to dinner. I picked these up from William's cabin before we left." Donna produced two bottles of tablets from her handbag, each with Eileen's name on the label and each half empty. "Do you think we could get the Infirmary to check them?"

"Not sure whether the Infirmary could do it, but I'm sure they can pass them on to the authorities in New York," replied Carol. "The Infirmary will be closed now, so let's take them down first thing in the morning."

"That sounds like a plan," said Donna, draining her gin. "Come on, let's go and see who comes to dinner."

Chapter 26

Alone in his cabin, William started packing Eileen's clothes into her suitcase.

No point in hanging about, he reasoned. *They can go with her when she leaves the ship tomorrow and I'll deal with them back in the UK.*

I suppose I'd better phone the children and let them know their mum's dead. They'll have to make the arrangements at home.

I'm not really sure how I feel right now, probably in a bit of shock. I'm bound to feel a bit sad, after all I've been married to the woman for well over thirty years. But now I'm a free man. I'll wait a suitable period of time of course, and then I'm going to make some major changes to my life.

Will those changes include Jenny? Mmm, not sure. I've known her a long time, ever since she took the secretary's job at the practice. Must be at least twenty years ago. I knew Jenny wanted more than friendship and if she hadn't drunk so much at the Christmas party a few years back and thrown herself at me, she would never have got her wish. Why did she have to complicate everything?

Yeah, we've enjoyed some good times together, but she's really not my type. She's so quiet and mousey, never engages with others and never starts a conversation. Come to think of it, I've never seen her really laugh, not like those other women at the dinner table. Now they know how to have a good time. I've only ever seen a spark of life in Jenny when we're in bed.

Maybe it's time to go our separate ways.

Right, that's Eileen's clothes sorted, just the toiletries now and someone from the team can come and collect them.

Better grab her medication before I forget. Oh God, where's she put it? I'm sure it was here earlier. I wonder if that doctor has picked it up? He's got no bloody right to do that. I'll check with him later.

Right, better get ready for dinner. I'm feeling quite hungry.

Chapter 27

"Sorry we're late, everyone," said Donna as they arrived at their dinner table, "we seem to be making a habit of it." She heard Carol laughing behind her, their dinner companions looking at them aghast.

"Yes, sorry. We got delayed in the Gin Bar. Donna's fault, she ordered large gins."

"I'm sorry, ladies, but William's had some bad news," said Alan, trying to quieten the four of them.

"Oh really?" said Carol, sitting next to William and placing a hand on his arm. She didn't want him to know that Fiona had already told them, didn't want him to think they were gossiping about him.

"Yes," replied William, "I'm sorry to say that Eileen passed away this afternoon."

"Oh my God," exclaimed Jess, "that's awful. I'm so sorry, William."

"Thank you," said William, looking sombre.

"What happened, William?" asked Carol.

"I went back to the cabin to check on her after lunch and she was dead."

"Had she been ill?" asked Win. "I thought she seemed fine over the first few days."

"She had a heart condition," replied William. "She'd been complaining a bit about palpitations and feeling sick, but we put that down to a touch of seasickness. I'm sure her heart must have simply given up."

"So what happens now?" asked Sue.

"Her body will be taken ashore in New York, where a death certificate will be issued and then she will be flown home."

"God, you must be devastated," Sue responded. "Is there anything any of us can do?"

"Thank you, that's very kind but no, there's nothing anyone can do. The team here on the ship are taking care of everything."

"You must be very upset too, Jenny. You must have known Eileen very well," said Fiona.

"Yes," replied Jenny, looking down at her folded hands resting in her lap.

"I expect you'll both be leaving us when we dock," said Win.

"No, on the contrary," replied William. "I've decided to remain in order to fulfil my lecture commitments. I can't let everyone down, especially when they look forward to hearing me speak."

Donna nudged Fiona under the table and gave her the 'told you so' look.

"Really?" said Sue. "Don't you want to fly home with your wife? I'm sure everyone will understand."

"No, honestly, I'll be fine."

Dinner was quite a gloomy affair. Nobody wanted to be too cheerful and upset William, but neither did they want to eat in silence. They ended up exchanging inane banter before Win broke the ice saying that he was heading off to finalise his talk for the following day.

"Right, we're off too," declared Donna, eager to get away. "We've got a few things to do, but if anyone fancies joining us we'll be in the Gin Bar from nine o'clock."

"What things have we got to do?" asked Fiona as the pair made their way out of the dining room.

"Nothing. I just couldn't face sitting there any longer listening to William. Sorry, Fi, but nothing that comes out of that man's mouth rings true to me."

"I know what you mean, Don, there is something about him but I'm not sure what. He sounds very plausible and I think the others all believe him. Do you think it's worth having a word with the security guy?"

"Not sure really. I mean, what is there to go on? We have a woman with a heart condition who's just died, probably from a heart attack, which her GP husband confirms. It's just us who's suspicious."

"Suspicious of what?" asked Carol, as she and Jess caught them up outside the toilets.

"William," said Fiona. "Donna still has these feelings about him and to be honest, Carol, I don't think they should be ignored. We were just talking about whether we should go and talk to Pete, the security officer."

"You could," she replied, "but I'm not sure he will treat it seriously. There's nothing to go on, only your gut feeling, Donna. Which, by the way, I'm not poo-pooing, but security will want concrete evidence of some sort."

"Why not take the medication to the Infirmary in the morning and see what that brings back?" said Jess. "Mum, I'm just nipping in here to the loo."

"She's got a good point," said Fiona. "If the tablets are anything other than what they're supposed to be, then we have some evidence to take to Pete."

"Right, that's a plan then," agreed Donna.

"Except that I've got a talk first thing in the morning, so can you do that one on your own?"

"Of course," replied Donna. "It shouldn't take too long and then I'll come and meet you in the theatre. The main thing will be getting someone to agree to test them."

"I'll come with you to the Infirmary, Donna," said Carol. "I'm sure between us we can persuade them to do what we want."

"Right, where we off to?" said Jess as she came out of the toilets.

"Gin Bar," the three women chorused.

Chapter 28

Carol was already waiting outside the Infirmary when Donna showed up the following morning.

"Ready?" she asked, pushing open the heavy blue door.

"Yes," said Donna, "let's do this."

Quite a few people were waiting patiently, the medical staff bustling about dealing with their relatively minor issues. Donna and Carol took seats, trying to memorise who was before them when they walked in. Eventually it was their turn to be seen.

"Who's next?" called a young nurse.

"She's the one who came out to Eileen yesterday," said Donna as they stood up and followed her through to a treatment room.

"Have I treated you before?" the nurse asked Donna.

"No, but I saw you yesterday when you responded to Eileen Mitchell's death. I'm Donna."

"Of course, I remember you now. So sad and my condolences. I'm Debbie, what can I do for you ladies this morning?"

"It's about Eileen actually," Carol responded. "We have concerns over the cause of her death and wonder if we can get her medication checked." Donna retrieved the two brown pill bottles from her shoulder bag.

"We know Eileen had a heart condition and was taking medication. But I have two bottles of tablets here, both the same drug but each bottle half full. Normally you finish one bottle before starting the next, so I'm wondering whether they are two different drugs."

"OK," said Debbie, reaching out to take the bottles from Donna. She read the labels, unscrewed the cap on the first bottle and shook a couple of pills into her hand.

"That's odd," she said. "This drug is usually a little round tablet, but these are quite large and oblong. It's also a bit odd that they're in bottles, medication nowadays usually comes in blister packs."

"Is there any way these can be tested?" asked Carol.

"We don't have the facilities on board, but any pharmaceutical lab should be able to do it. Why? What are your thoughts?"

"I'm wondering if Eileen might have taken an overdose, but that depends on what the drugs are."

"I guess that's feasible," said the nurse. "What I can do is send these off with Eileen and request that the authorities in New York test them."

"That would be great, thank you," replied Donna.

"Would it also be possible to take some of Eileen's blood and get that tested too?" asked Carol. "That would rule out an overdose, wouldn't it?"

"Yes, that's possible, but I would have to check with the doctor that I can do it. But tell me, ladies, I'm sensing that you don't think Eileen's death is natural."

"Let's just say knowing her death was from natural causes would give us peace of mind," replied Donna.

"OK," replied the nurse, "I'll see what I can do."

Chapter 29

The energy around the ship had risen a notch or two on the final day at sea before their first stop. Passengers were excited to get off the ship for the first time in six days and into New York. Crossing the Atlantic Ocean had been relatively smooth, but the captain wasn't particularly helpful by constantly informing everyone that they were crossing the area where the *Titanic* sunk. He also had a penchant for mentioning the Bermuda Triangle, although they were nowhere near it.

"Do you think the Bermuda Triangle really exists?" Fiona asked Donna as they relaxed with a couple of cappuccinos after her talk.

"Yeah, I do. I've no idea what it is but loads of ships and planes have mysteriously disappeared there. I'd like to think it's a portal into another world, or another time."

"Bloody hell, Don, you've been watching too many sci-fi movies. They're just stories from someone's overactive imagination."

"But who's to say they're not real? The imagination has to be triggered by something. I think it was Picasso who once said 'everything you can imagine is real'."

"Jeez, Donna, sometimes you frighten me with all this stuff."

"You shouldn't be frightened by it, Fi. There is so much in this life, this world and even the universe that we know nothing about. I want to find out all I can."

"Hello, ladies," said Win, as he appeared at their table. "Do you mind if I join you for coffee?"

"Of course not," said Fiona, pulling out a chair. "We were just talking about the Bermuda Triangle that the captain is so fond of mentioning. Do you think it exists?"

"I believe something exists. There are too many coincidences of ships and aircraft that go missing in that area and are never traced."

"Donna thinks it's a portal to another world," laughed Fiona.

"Don't rule it out," smiled Win. "Some say it's the Gateway to Atlantis."

"See!" exclaimed Donna. "Keep an open mind. Anything is possible until proven otherwise."

"OK, OK," laughed Fiona, arms raised and palms outward in submission. "Point taken."

"Changing the subject," said Win. "What do you ladies think about Eileen's death?"

"Jury's still out," replied Donna.

"It seems all a bit odd to me too," Win continued. "William seems his normal self after he's just lost his wife."

"Maybe they didn't get on and he's happy that it's over," Fiona responded.

"Perhaps," said Win, "after all, he does have his secretary to take his mind off things."

"Do you think they're having an affair?" asked Donna.

"Highly likely, why else would he bring her? You certainly don't need a secretary to give a few talks. Anyway, you women are far more perceptive in picking up these things, what do you think?"

"I think they are," replied Donna. "The only thing that's a bit odd is that she doesn't seem a good match for him. He's so outgoing and full of himself and she's so quiet, a little mouse in comparison. Fiona thinks he chose her because she allows him to shine."

"Yeah, that's a fair comment," he replied. "So what have you two got planned in the Big Apple?"

"Sightseeing, shopping and tomorrow night we have booked a dinner show with live music from a blues band. What are you doing?" asked Fiona.

"Sightseeing for sure, there's just so much to see. Right," Win said, pushing his chair back, "must go, I've got my next talk in half an hour."

Chapter 30

The queue to disembark was already a long one when Donna and Fiona joined the back. Preferring to do their own thing, they headed for the complimentary shuttle bus that would take them straight to Times Square.

"What shall we do first?" asked Donna as she settled into her seat.

"Why don't we start at the bottom and work up? If you want to do the Statue of Liberty, then we need to get down to Battery Park and take the ferry. Then we can head back up and do Ground Zero."

"Sounds good to me, but I worry we'll run out of time."

"We probably will," laughed Fiona, "but if we concentrate on seeing the things on the top of our list today, we can shop tomorrow and if we have any time left we can finish off the sightseeing. It's a shame we're only here for one night."

"We do have a stop on the way back, but we won't cover much in a day. I know they have open-top bus tours so maybe that would be a good way to see a lot of places," said Donna.

"Yes, and there's also a boat trip around Manhattan Island, so we can see a different side of the city."

As the bus finally pulled over in the centre of Manhattan, the driver quickly grabbed the microphone before his passengers made their bid for freedom.

"Listen up, people," he called above the excited chatter. "Remember this location, write it down, take photos. We're right in the heart of Times Square, near the junction of 42nd and 7th. Shuttle buses leave every hour on the hour and run throughout the night. Take care and have fun, people."

He opened the door and his passengers spewed off in a never-ending stream, gathering on the pavement, looking around in wonder and confusion.

"Where do we get a bus to Battery Park?" asked Fiona, as they moved towards the exit.

"Port Authority right over there, ma'am," he said, pointing across the street. "But your best and cheapest option would be Big Bus Tours, then you can hop on and off wherever you like. Red line covers downtown, and the blue line is for uptown."

"Thank you so much," said Fiona. "You've been really helpful."

"You're welcome, ma'am. Have a nice day."

A red Big Bus was already waiting at the stop. The girls waved, ran and jumped on before it had time to move off. They bought two-day flexible passes and made their way to the open deck upstairs.

They studied the map the driver gave them, circling the stops where they needed to get off.

At Battery Park they stood in line for the ferry and bought combined tickets for the Statue of Liberty and Ellis Island. The ferry trip was short, which was just as well as they were packed in like sardines. Fiona had to wonder how many passengers were crammed in and whether they had exceeded maximum capacity.

"My word, this is a lot bigger than it appears at a distance," said Fiona, as she peered up at the impressive statue.

"It says here that it was a gift from France to the people of the United States back in the late eighteen hundreds to signify freedom and liberty," said Donna, reading from one of the plaques.

"Some gift," said Fiona. "Wonder why it's green when it's made from copper."

"Probably standing out in all weathers for hundreds of years."

They toyed with the idea of going up to the viewing platform in the crown, but the hundred-and-sixty-step climb quickly put them off. Instead, they wandered around its base, enjoying the view across the Hudson River from a different angle.

After a coffee and the obligatory mooch around the gift shop, they headed back towards the ferry stop and a quick ride across to Ellis Island.

"Oh wow!" exclaimed Donna, standing and gazing around her. "This place has so much history. Can you believe it was the first place thousands of immigrants came to when they arrived in the States?"

"When was that?" Fiona asked.

"Sometime in the eighteen hundreds I think. Do you know what, Fi?" Donna said. "I think I might research my family when we get home. I don't know much about my grandparents, and nothing about my great-grandparents."

"Really?"

"Yeah. How amazing would it be to know that I've stood in the same room that one of my ancestors did?"

"I suppose so," replied Fiona, "but I bet it's not easy to do."

"Probably not, but I'm going to try. There's several websites out there now that can help with family history stuff, so that's where I'll start."

Their next stop was Ground Zero. They joined the many tourists who stood in silence, paying their respects to those who lost their lives that awful day. The memorial was both beautiful and emotional. Donna sensed the fear and desperation of those who died in the attack, and the grief of those waiting patiently for news of loved ones.

"Can you smell it, Don?" whispered Fiona. "That burning smell is still here."

"Yes, I can. It's truly awful isn't it? Why people carry out such atrocious acts is beyond me. Why on earth can't we all live in peace and harmony?"

"Didn't al-Qaeda claim it? They are an extremist group that clearly have no boundaries. Human life means nothing to them."

"I understand that we all have different beliefs and opinions, but why can't we all agree to disagree without such violence?"

"I don't know, darling," said Fiona. The two girls stood with their arms around one another, allowing the tears to fall, remembering the victims of the attack.

Back on the bus they enjoyed the sights, sounds and even the smells as they drove past the Empire State Building and the Flatiron Building. They rode through Greenwich Village and Soho, saw Wall Street and all the other landmarks that they had seen in films or read about in books. They ended their bus tour at Circle Line Sightseeing Cruises and took a boat tour around Manhattan Island, where their guide pointed out more famous landmarks.

"Jeez Fi, I'm knackered," said Donna. "We've crammed so much in today."

"I know, and it's been amazing. It's gone seven o'clock," said Fiona, looking at her watch. "Shall we make our way over to the music hall now? By the time we get there, they should be open."

"Yes. We can at least sit down and have a drink or three."

Chapter 31

Sitting at the bar in the music venue, Donna kicked off her sandals and rubbed her tired feet.

"God knows how far we've walked today, must be miles."

"All good exercise though," replied Fiona. "Means we can enjoy dessert now without feeling too guilty."

"Never feel guilty if you enjoy it. Life's too short to give up on pleasures."

"Hello," said a deep, velvety voice behind her. "Can we buy you two ladies a drink?"

Donna looked up at Fiona. Her face a picture with an open mouth and wide-eyed stare of someone who'd just had a seizure. Donna swivelled on her bar stool, her eyes resting on a muscular torso clad in a tight white T-shirt. Her gaze travelled upwards, taking in the broad shoulders, bronzed muscular arms and a face too handsome to be true. What's more, there were two of them. She swivelled back to Fiona.

"Oh my God," she mouthed, before quickly turning back to the strangers behind her.

"That would be lovely, thank you. Two gin and tonics, please."

"You're English?" said guy number two, signalling for the bartender.

"Yes, we are," Donna replied.

"Well it's lovely to meet two beautiful English roses," said guy number one. "I'm Aaron and this is my twin brother, Jacob."

"I'm Donna and this is my mute friend Fiona." Donna swung around and shot Fiona a 'for heaven's sake, get a grip' look as she still sat staring open-mouthed.

They sipped their drinks and chatted until an announcement asked those with dinner reservations to take their seats.

"I'm sorry, but we have to go now," said Fiona, who had finally found her voice.

"Let's meet up after the show," said Aaron. "We can have a few more drinks and get to know each other a little better."

Donna smiled as the two of them left the bar and headed off to find their table. It was in a prime spot, two rows back and centre stage. The act was a blues band, well known in the States, but not in the UK.

"You know what they're after, don't you, Donna?" said Fiona, after they had placed their food choices with the waitress.

"Of course, they're hardly subtle about it are they? We'll have to make our escape as quickly as we can after the show."

The show was brilliant as the band played a range of well-known songs. Donna was in her element, singing, clapping and moving to the music. The lack of a dance floor was her only criticism. Fiona silently thanked those who needed thanking for this design oversight.

As the show came to an end, Donna glanced around and saw the twins waiting at the end of the aisle. They had no other way out but to walk past them.

"Did you enjoy the show, ladies?" asked Jacob, as the girls drew level.

"Yes, it was brilliant," replied Donna.

"Good. Well the bar is open for another hour so there's time for one more drink," said Aaron in his deep southern drawl. "Gin and tonic, ladies?"

"Actually," said Fiona, "I think I would like a brandy to round off the evening." Donna nodded in agreement.

"Ahh but the night is young," said Jacob, as they placed their orders with the bartender.

"It is," replied Donna, "but we've had a full day of sightseeing and are absolutely knackered."

"I just love the way you girls talk," said Aaron.

I bet you do, thought Donna as she took a large gulp of her brandy.

"I'm just off to the ladies, won't be long," she said, as Fiona stared at her in alarm at being left alone.

Five minutes later and Fiona's phone chirped with an incoming message from Donna.

Toilets. Now.

"I'm sorry," she said, reading it quickly. "Donna needs me, be right back."

Chapter 32

"Donna," called Fiona as she pulled open the door to the ladies.

"In here," Donna called back. Fiona heard movement and banging from one of the stalls and moved towards it. Tapping on the outside of the door she called softly.

"Donna, are you in there?"

"I'm locked in. I can't open the door," Donna said, banging and rattling on it.

"How the bloody hell did you manage that?" Fiona asked, her eyes rolled up in disbelief.

"Long story, but I had to adjust the lock when I came in and now I'm stuck. You have to get me out of here."

"For God's sake, Donna, you certainly do some stupid things in."

"I didn't do it on purpose."

"But why did you have to fiddle with the lock in the first place?"

"Because the door didn't shut properly and I didn't want anyone barging in."

"But there's no-one in here."

"Not now there isn't, but someone might come in."

Fiona laughed.

"It's not funny, Fiona. Stop laughing and get me out of here."

Fiona tried fiddling with the lock from the outside, but it was jammed solid.

"It's no good, Donna, it's not working. Maybe I should go and get someone, perhaps the twins can help?"

"Don't you dare," snarled Donna. "Try again."

"OK, stand well back and I'll see if putting a bit of weight behind it might work."

After a lot of pushing and running at the door, Fiona gave up. Her shoulder was beginning to hurt and she didn't have the strength to push any more.

"It's not working, Don, time for Plan B."

"What's that?"

"Either I need to go and get the twins or you need to climb over the top and into the next cubicle."

"Do not bring the twins in here, I'll climb over."

Donna started banging and crashing around in the cubicle.

"What on earth are you doing?" called Fiona.

"I can't reach the top just standing on the toilet, so I've moved the bin over. It's a bit wobbly but at least I can just about get to the top."

Fiona went into the next cubicle just as Donna's hands and the top of her head appeared over the partition.

"I'm going to heave myself up on the count of three, just be ready to steady me."

Fiona waited as she heard Donna count to three. The partition shook under her weight, the bin crashed away from under her feet and Donna was left stranded. Balancing on her waist, her head and arms in the new cubicle, her bottom half dangling in the locked one.

"Shit Fi, I'm stuck!" she wailed. With nothing to grab hold of and nothing to push her feet against, Donna resembled a beached whale trying to perfect its yoga moves. Fiona tried hard to stifle her laughter as she looked up at the flailing arms. "Oh hell, there's someone coming in," she said as she heard voices.

"Perhaps they could help," replied Fiona, trying hard not to laugh.

"Stop bloody laughing and get me down," Donna yelled.

"Hang on, let me just get a picture," Fiona laughed.

"You do and you and me are finished, lady," threatened Donna.

"Don't worry, I'd never do that to you," Fiona chuckled. "Now keep still, I'm going to pull you over, but when I start pulling try and get your legs higher than your body and we'll let gravity do its thing."

"You can't do that, I'm too heavy."

"We don't have a choice, unless you want the twins in here?"

"No I don't! Let's give it a go."

"Right, ready?" As Fiona started pulling, Donna raised her legs as high as she could get them and eventually reached the tipping point. She slid down into Fiona's arms and with a lot of grunting and groaning got her feet down onto the floor.

"Bloody hell," grunted Fiona, taking Donna's weight. "Please don't ever do that again."

"Fi, you're covered in blood. Where did that come from?"

"It must be from you," Fiona took Donna's hands and found a nasty gash across the palm of one of them. "Look."

"I thought something hurt as I pulled myself up but was too busy concentrating on getting over the top."

"You'd better go and wash it, who knows what germs are lurking in here and the last thing you want is an infection," said Fiona, trying to pull the door inwards so they could both get out.

They left the cubicle to a round of applause. A few women had gathered. Enthralled by the spectacle they stood watching Donna slide over the top of the partition.

"Thank you," said Donna, bowing graciously, "I'm afraid that cubicle is out of action."

Without any explanation Donna washed and dried her hand and pressed a clean paper towel into her palm, her audience dispersing into the empty toilets.

"Right Fi, let's get out of here."

Fiona opened the door then slammed it quickly and stepped back into the washroom.

"The twins are just outside. Looks like they're waiting for us."

"Bloody hell, they don't give up do they?" said Donna.

"No, but then they think they're onto a good thing. Probably anticipating a foursome," said Fiona. "Right," she said, moving across to the towel dispenser and pulling out handfuls. "Let's wrap your hand in these, and then support your arm with the other one."

"Blimey, Fi," said Donna, looking down at her hand. "You sure you've used enough?"

"Let's go," said Fiona, opening the door again and spying the twins in the same position. "Let me do the talking. I've got a plan, and you're in pain."

"Fi, I don't think this is a good idea."

"Have you got a better one?"

"No."

"Come on then, let's get out of here."

"There you are," said Aaron, the smile on his face rapidly fading when he caught sight of Donna. "What happened to you?"

"I found Donna lying on the floor," Fiona explained. "She's got a really nasty wound and her wrist could be broken. I've stabilised it for now, but I need to get her to a hospital."

If the twins felt any disappointment, it was only fleetingly. Donna caught sight of Aaron moving towards a couple of blondes who were just about to leave.

As soon as they were outside, Fiona retrieved her phone and quickly found directions towards the stop for the shuttle bus to take them back to the ship.

"Are you heading back to the cruise ships?" mouthed Donna, rapping on the window of the waiting bus.

"Yes, ma'am," said the driver, opening the door. "I can't depart until one am, but climb aboard and make yourselves comfortable. Looks like you ladies had a good evening," he said, staring at Donna's mummified hand.

"Let's say it was interesting," replied Fiona, pushing Donna down the bus.

Chapter 33

Surprisingly, the girls were up early the following morning and, after grabbing some toast and a quick cup of tea from the cafeteria, made their way off the ship and back to the shuttle bus. Another day in New York and they were determined to make the most of it.

Crossing the street, they waited for the Big Bus on the blue route to take them around uptown Manhattan. The tour didn't seem to take so long as the red route the previous day, but they enjoyed the views from the east side of Central Park.

Leaving the bus they made their way back to the music hall for their booking for Brunch with the Harlem Gospel Choir.

"I hope the twins don't show up this morning," said Fiona, as they waited in the queue to go into the main hall.

"Me too," said Donna, "but when we left last night, one of them was eyeing up a couple of blondes. As gorgeous as they are, I can't be doing with all that malarky."

"Me neither, and as much as I love you, I don't have the urge to sleep with you," said Fiona.

"Really?" laughed Donna, winking at her friend. "I don't know why."

"Hopefully they had better luck with the blondes. Mind you, they wasted a fair bit of money on drinks for us."

"Ahh, but that's the name of the game. Some you win, some you lose."

The doors opened and people filed in, looking for their table numbers. Brunch was a self-service buffet with a wide selection of food, some of which Donna had never heard of. They made their choices and headed back to their table, tucking into their lunch feast.

The auditorium erupted as the choir made their way onto the stage. Dressed in black, the women with long dresses and the men in shirts and trousers, but all with a gold sash draped around their necks. Their singing was phenomenal as they belted out a range of songs and hymns. The audience sang and clapped along and of course, Donna was having a wonderful time.

The show ended all too quickly and they were back on the street. They had one last booking before they needed to head back to the shuttle bus. The last bus left at four o'clock, allowing plenty of time to get all passengers back on board for their five o'clock deadline and a six o'clock sailing.

The girls headed over to the helipad where they had booked a helicopter ride over Manhattan. After a safety briefing, their pilot led them out to the helicopter and quickly strapped them into their little yellow life-jackets, no more than a small backpack resting on their chests. The two other couples joining them pushed their way to the front, eager to be first on board to claim the front seats. But first on board were forced into the back seats and Donna's and Fiona's patience was rewarded with the two prized seats next to the pilot.

Large oval headphones covered the whole of the ear and helped deaden the noise of the engine and rotor blades, but allowed the commentary from the pilot to be heard.

The helicopter rose into the air, wobbled a bit before it banked to the left and headed up the west side of the Hudson River. The views from the front window were spectacular.

About thirty minutes later, the pilot brought the chopper back to the helipad, ending the tour.

"That," said Fiona, as they made their way back to the building, "has got to be the main highlight of this trip. Who'd have thought Central Park would be so huge?"

"I know," Donna replied. "It's unbelievable really, that for a small island there is so much crammed in."

"I must have taken hundreds of photos, but God knows what they'll turn out like with all that vibration going on," laughed Fiona.

"Me too. But it almost doesn't matter that they won't be perfect, they're our memories no matter what."

"I guess we'd better make our way back to the shuttle bus now," said Fiona. "We don't want to miss the last one."

Chapter 34

"Fi, have a look at my hand, will you?" said Donna the following morning.

"Why, what's the matter?" replied Fiona, pulling open the curtains across the balcony doors. The ocean and clear blue sky stretched before them as they continued their journey down to the Caribbean.

"It feels really quite sore this morning." Donna moved across to the window so Fiona had a better view in the daylight.

"Ooooh, I don't like the look of that," said Fiona, as she inspected the angry looking wound and the puffiness around the area. "Come on, it's down to the Infirmary for you."

They took their seats and waited for someone to call them. It was quiet in the medical centre, and it wasn't too long before the door to the treatment room opened, discharging a satisfied patient.

"Hello, Donna," said Debbie, the duty nurse. "What can I do for you this morning?"

"It's my hand. I got it caught the day before yesterday and today it's really feeling sore."

"Come in and let's take a look."

"Is it OK if Fiona comes in too?"

"Sure, if it's OK with you then it's OK with me. Take a seat on the edge of the couch; Fiona, there's a chair over there for you."

Debbie examined Donna's hand and noticed how she winced when she touched certain areas.

"What did you catch this on? Was it dirty?"

"It was the top of a partition in the ladies' toilets and yes, I imagine it was extremely filthy," Fiona chipped in before Donna could spin her own story on the events in the club two nights ago.

"The top of a partition? Do you mean between two toilets?" asked Debbie, surprise registering on her face.

"Yes," Fiona continued. "I needed to get Donna out of the toilet and she scraped her hand as she climbed over the top."

"Wouldn't it have been easier to simply leave by the door?" asked Debbie, intrigued as to why Donna would feel it necessary to climb her way out, and clearly wanting to know more. Neither of the girls felt the need to explain further.

"It looks like your hand has become slightly infected, which is not too surprising considering where you were. I'll clean the wound, spread some antibiotic ointment over the open areas and cover with a dressing. Is that OK?"

"Thanks, Debbie," said Donna, nodding in agreement.

"I hope the ointment will do the job rather than put you on a course of antibiotics, but I want to see you again in the morning to check and see how things are looking."

"OK," replied Donna. "By the way, have you heard back from anyone about Eileen Mitchell's medication and her blood results?"

"Yes, we have. Not sure I should be telling you this, but I know you girls have a few concerns over her death. The medication was potassium chloride and there were exceedingly high levels of it in her blood."

"Bloody hell," said Donna, looking across at Fiona.

"Were those high levels enough to kill her?" asked Fiona.

"They could certainly contribute to inducing a heart attack, especially as she had a heart condition anyway."

"So let's be clear," said Donna. "Could this be murder?"

"Can't rule it out," Debbie replied.

Chapter 35

As Carol finished her morning talk she saw Donna waving frantically from the back of the theatre. She gave a thumbs up sign in acknowledgement and quickly thanked her audience, giving details of when she would be speaking again.

"What's up?" she asked, as she breathlessly ran up the stairs and joined them at the entrance.

"Developments," said Donna. "Where's Jess?"

"She's around somewhere, she should be here soon. What's happened to your hand?" asked Carol, noticing the dressing the nurse had just applied.

"Long story," laughed Fiona, "which is probably best shared over a drink."

"OK," said Carol, a frown of enquiry on her face. "Here comes Jess now."

"Morning, you two," said Jess.

"Let's go somewhere quiet, we need to talk."

"What... ?" Jess started to ask, glancing down at Donna's bandaged hand but caught the shake of her mother's head which simply said 'don't ask'. Mothers the world over seemed to be exceptionally good at giving looks, especially to their spouses and children. Just one look would convey many words, ignore them at your peril.

They found a table in a quiet area in the Lido Restaurant. Too late for breakfast and too early for lunch, there was just a handful of people enjoying a morning coffee. The four women grabbed their own drinks and sat down, waiting for Donna to enlighten them.

"This morning we went to the Infirmary about Donna's hand," Fiona started. "Don't ask what she's done, we'll share that story later."

"Luckily I saw Debbie, and she told us that the results were back on Eileen's medication and blood test. Evidently, the pills she'd been taking were potassium chloride, plus there were exceedingly high levels of it in her bloodstream."

"Potassium chloride affects the muscles in the heart and high levels of it can cause palpitations, arrhythmias, weakness in the arms and legs, nausea and vomiting and other stuff but, more importantly, could lead to a heart attack," said Donna.

"Shit," said Carol. "So are we looking at murder?"

"Debbie would only say that it couldn't be ruled out," continued Donna. "But I think we have to look at it closely, don't you?"

"Yes, I do," replied Carol.

"I presume William and Jenny are still on board?" asked Jess. "I haven't seen either of them since we arrived in New York."

"Not seen them either," said Fiona.

"I'm sure they are," Donna said, "but I think we need to make sure."

"What else can we do?" asked Jess. "After all, this is just one blood sample that I'm guessing we shouldn't even know about. We can't suddenly accuse the man of murdering his wife."

"No we can't," said Carol, "but there are things we can do."

"Like what?" asked Fiona.

"Well, if we were home right now, I would run a background check on him."

"I could ask Matt to do that," said Donna, looking over at Fiona for confirmation.

"Agreed," she said. "Matt is a very good friend who's helped us in the past. His partner is a freelance investigative journalist, so I'm guessing he has access to all sorts of databases."

"What else can we do?" asked Donna.

"Not much more at this stage," replied Carol. "I think our priority is to make sure William and Jenny are still on the ship. Jess and I can do that."

"OK, then I'll get the boys on a background check, and also look at both William and Jenny, just to be on the safe side. I mean, we're assuming that if Eileen was murdered, he did it. It could have been Jenny."

"True," said Carol.

"I also think a chat with Pete, the security guy, wouldn't go amiss. I'm happy to do that, seeing as we've already met."

"OK then, that all sounds good to me. Let's get on with things and then have a catch-up later," said Carol, rising from her chair.

"Okey doke," said Fiona, "see you both later. Right babe, shall we go in search of Pete?"

Chapter 36

Fiona and Donna made their way down to the Concierge Desk on the lower deck. As usual the large queue of guests who had viewed their on-line accounts were querying the vast quantities of alcohol that had been added, all of which they mysteriously forgot drinking, made for a long wait.

"Good morning, how can I help?" said a pleasant receptionist when they reached the front.

"We'd like to see Pete, the security officer. Where would we find him?" asked Donna.

"Is it something I can help you with, madam?"

"No, it isn't. Sorry, that's nothing against you, it's just we've already been speaking with Pete."

"OK, well in that case have a seat over there and I'll give him a call. Can I just take your name please?"

"Yes, it's Donna Chambers. Tell him it's about Eileen Mitchell."

"What are you doing now?" asked Fiona, sitting in a comfy chair in the central lobby and watching her friend whip out her mobile phone.

"I'm going to have to connect to the internet so I can message Matt," Donna replied. "Bloody hell, these prices are extortionate, how on earth can they justify that?"

Eventually connected, Donna sent Matt a brief message.

Matt, need help.

Can you run background checks on a Dr William Mitchell, retired GP in Berkshire. Wife Eileen, secretary Jenny Jones. Need info ASAP, get Jason to help.

Love D xxx

"There, that's got the ball rolling," she said, putting her phone back in her pocket.

Five minutes later Pete walked through a door behind reception. Nodding to the receptionist as she pointed across to where the pair were sitting, he walked quickly towards them.

"Hello, ladies, I believe you wanted to see me."

"Yes," said Donna, taking the lead. "There have been developments in the Eileen Mitchell case. Is there somewhere more private we can talk?"

"OK, you'd better come into my office."

He led them through a door at the side of Reception, down a corridor and opened a door on the left.

"Please, have a seat. Now, what are these new developments?"

"Before we docked in New York we asked one of the medical team whether they could check Eileen's medication. She said the contents of the bottles did not match the description on the label. Whilst they are not equipped to do the testing on board, she said she would send it ashore with Eileen."

Pete nodded throughout Fiona's explanation.

"We also asked if a blood sample could be taken and tested at the same time," added Donna.

"And was that done?" asked Pete.

"Yes, it was."

"This morning we checked if the results were back," continued Fiona. "Apparently the pill bottles contained potassium chloride and not the digoxin on the labels. Additionally, Eileen's blood showed high levels of potassium in her system."

"Potassium, when taken in excess, can induce a heart attack and subsequently, death," added Donna.

"I see," said Pete. "So are you saying that someone swapped her medication, hoping to end her life?"

"Yes, that's exactly what I'm saying."

"Could she not have been taking the potassium hoping to end her own life?"

"What? Suicide, you mean?" yelled Donna. "No way."

"But you can't be sure, can you?"

"No, not one hundred per cent, no. But if she wanted to end her own life why on earth would she make it a long and painful process, and where would she get the drug from? There are much better, and easier ways to take your own life. In my own mind I'm absolutely certain this was not suicide," Donna said, getting quite cross that Pete was not taking this seriously enough. "Can't you pull William in for questioning?"

"No, Donna, I'm afraid I can't. I hear what you're saying, but I have no real evidence that he may have been involved in the death of his wife."

"But what about her pills and blood test? Does that count for nothing?" Fiona could sense Donna was becoming quite shirty. It was something she did when she felt people were not really listening to her or taking her seriously.

"Donna," she said, "I think it's time to leave now. Clearly we're getting nowhere fast."

The girls stood and moved to the door, but Donna had to have the final word.

"I'll find the evidence. One way or another, I will find it and then, Mr Head of Security, you will eat your words."

Donna slammed the door behind her and let out a loud yell in the corridor.

"It's no good you getting arsy, babe," said Fiona, "it's not going to help."

"I know, but it aggravates me when people are not listening."

"Ahh but to be fair, he doesn't have the level of intuition that you have. Let's wait and see what Matt comes up with, if anything."

Chapter 37

William and Jenny were at dinner that evening.

"Hello, William, Jenny, how are you both doing?" asked Sue as she prepared to take her place.

"Oh not so bad, under the circumstances," replied William. "I think I just need time for the whole nightmare to sink in."

"I'm sure you do," said Alan, Sue's husband. "It must have come as quite a shock."

"What happens now?" asked Win.

"The authorities back in New York are dealing with everything and will eventually send her home. I have messaged my children telling them to make arrangements with a funeral director if I'm not back."

"So there's nothing more you can do until you get back to the UK?"

"No Win, I just have to wait now."

"How about you, Jenny?" asked Sue. "This must be a terrible shock for you too. How are you coping?"

"OK," mumbled Jenny, looking down at her hands folded in her lap.

Blimey, thought Donna, *hard to imagine that one having wild, passionate sex with William. Hard to imagine William for that matter.* She tried to stifle a laugh that was bubbling up.

The remainder of dinner was quite subdued. Nobody felt it appropriate to laugh and joke and as soon as coffee was finished they each made their escape.

"What are you two doing this evening?" asked Jess.

"We'll do the show then probably head into the ballroom. What about you?" asked Fiona.

"Same," she replied.

"Great, might see you there later."

As the girls wandered along to the theatre, Donna checked her phone for messages. The internet was a bit hit and miss and she didn't want to miss anything from Matt.

His reply was waiting:

What the bloody hell are you two up to now?

Love M xx

"Matt wants to know what we're up to now," laughed Donna.

"You will have to tell him if we want his help," her friend replied.

Nothing much, just someone died and my intuition is telling me to look at the husband.

Don't tell Dave.

Love D xx

"Right," said Donna, linking her arm through Fiona's. "Let's go and have some fun, lady, and fingers crossed we'll have something back from the boys by the morning."

Chapter 38

"I wish this ship would get a move on," said Jenny, bustling about the cabin the following morning, clearing away some of William's mess. She had all but moved into his cabin after they left New York, leaving just a few bits and pieces in her own for appearances. It was the first time Jenny had spent any length of time alone with him, and if she was being honest, it wasn't how she imagined it would be.

"I need to be back on dry land now and put this whole thing behind us," she continued, slamming the wardrobe door.

"Don't you think I want this over and done with too?" said William, lying back on the bed and trying to read a book.

"Yes, I'm sure you do. But I am getting sick and tired of all the questions at dinner every night. Those women want to know far too much about us."

"I suppose a death on board has piqued their interest, especially with two of them running a detective agency."

"Why oh why couldn't she have died before we came on this trip? It would have made life so much easier."

"Yes, it would. But the fact is that she didn't, so we just have to get on with it."

"We could have enjoyed this trip so much more if we didn't have all this to deal with."

"Would you have ever enjoyed this trip, Jenny?" William slammed his book down on the bedside table and focussed his whole attention on her. "You've done nothing but moan since we got on board – first she's in the way and stopping us having fun and now that she's gone, she's still stopping us having fun. What do you actually want, Jenny?"

"I want us to be a couple, but I'm just seen as the secretary, the hanger-on."

"I'm sure that's not true. But you don't help yourself really, do you?"

"What do you mean?"

"You're not exactly chatty with our dinner companions, you sit there all the time with your head down staring into your lap. What are they supposed to think?"

"I don't care what they think," Jenny shouted.

"But you just moaned about them thinking you're only the secretary. You can't have it both ways, Jenny, make a bloody effort and engage with people. That's one thing Eileen was good at."

"Eileen, Eileen, Eileen, that's all I've heard since the day she died. Anyone would think you're missing her."

"I am missing her to some degree. I was married to the woman for years so you can't expect me not to feel a little emotional now she's gone."

"But you said you wanted her out of your life."

"I know I did, but the reality of it is totally different to wanting it."

"For God's sake, William, I don't know where I stand with you. The sooner we get home and out of this mess the better."

"Agreed. I need some space," said William, getting up from the bed and striding out of the cabin, slamming the door behind him.

Chapter 39

"Are these seats free?" asked a tall, distinguished looking man somewhere in his late fifties.

"Yes, please help yourself," said Donna, waving her arm toward the two vacant seats on the opposite side of the table. After the show, the girls headed towards the ballroom, where the resident band was playing a mix of well-known popular music. The band was just coming to the end of their set and the twenty-minute break gave everyone the opportunity to order another drink.

"Hello, my lady Donna and my lady Fiona," said Ryan, their gorgeous waiter. "Same again?"

"Yes please," said Donna, rummaging in her bag for her key card.

"Please, allow me," said the distinguished man, popping his key card on Ryan's tray and placing his own order.

"That's very kind of you," said Donna, "but there's really no need."

"It's my pleasure. I'm Tony by the way and this is my brother, James."

"Nice to meet you both," replied Donna, introducing herself and Fiona.

"Do you cruise often?" asked Fiona. "God, that was a cliché wasn't it?" she laughed, looking at Donna.

"Yeah, it was," Donna laughingly replied.

"No," laughed Tony, "this is our first cruise. I have no idea why we decided to do it, just seemed like a good idea at the time."

"Are you sorry to be here then?" asked Donna.

"Not at all," said James, "it's just that we're constantly taken as a couple of gay men."

"Nothing wrong with gay men," replied Fiona.

"Indeed not," said James. "I just feel it's assumed that two men holidaying together are gay, whereas two women are deemed to be friends or sisters."

"You could be right," said Donna, "I've never really thought about it to be honest. Fiona and I always have a holiday together every year, and enjoy our time together."

"Are you two a couple?" asked James.

"No, we're best friends, but we've known each other so long that we're more like sisters."

"This is the first holiday we've had together as just the two of us," said Tony. "James lost his wife last year and Sheila, my wife, suggested we spend some quality time together, just the two of us."

"That's very thoughtful of her," said Fiona.

"Yes, she's very caring and wants to see James happy again. Although we both realise that will take time."

"Yes, it will," replied Fiona, her thoughts turning to Nikos and how hard she found coping with his death and she wasn't even married to the man. "I lost my partner last year and the pain is only just beginning to lessen a bit. I guess it will never go away, but we'll learn to live with it."

"I hope so," said James.

"Would either of you care to dance?" asked Tony.

"Thank you," said Fiona, "I would love to."

"Please don't think I'm coming on to either of you," Tony laughed. "It just seems too good a moment to waste."

"It's fine," said Fiona. "Neither of us are here looking for romance, so a no strings attached drink and dance is perfect."

Carol and Jess had just arrived and began making their way around the edge of the dance floor, but when Jess saw Fiona dancing with a strange man she grabbed her mother's arm and veered her in the opposite direction.

"What are you doing?" asked Carol.

"Looks like the girls might have pulled," said Jess. "Best leave them to it."

Chapter 40

"How do we do it, Fi?" asked Donna, as they were preparing for bed. "We seem to have a knack for picking up random men."

"Don't knock it, babe, at least we can still do it," laughed Fiona. "The real knack is knowing how to knock them back without hurting their feelings."

"The two tonight were OK. Oh, I've got a reply from Matt."

"What's he say?" asked Fiona.

"Jason's found an old newspaper report about the death of a woman in a village close to Henley-on-Thames. It seems the post mortem was inconclusive, so the coroner requested an inquest. Get this, the husband was local GP, William James Mitchell."

"Bloody hell," said Fiona. "Do they have the outcome of the inquest?"

"He doesn't say, but I think this needs looking at further. I'd certainly like to know the cause of death."

"Would be good to know when they married and whether they had any children. How long after she died did he marry Eileen, I wonder."

"I'll ask the boys to find out," said Donna, tapping away on her phone.

"So are we thinking that he might have killed his first wife, and repeated it with Eileen?" asked Fiona.

"It's a possibility, isn't it?"

"Yeah, suppose it is, but we won't really know until we find out more. Then we have to get Security Pete to take it seriously."

"We need to do it all as soon as possible," replied Donna. "William could leave the ship any time and disappear."

"Do you think that's likely?" asked Fiona. "He said he was staying until we get back to Southampton."

"I think we'll be OK, unless he gets wind of us becoming suspicious, then who knows what he might do. But we do need to keep an eye on him."

"Not much more we can do until we hear back from Matt, is there?" said Fiona, stifling a yawn.

"No, there's not," Donna replied. "Let's get some sleep. We've got the catamaran trip tomorrow."

"I'm looking forward to that, it will be nice to have some time on a beach and dipping our toes in the ocean."

"Yes, it will. A lovely relaxing day, eh?"

Chapter 41

The ship docked in Dominica early the next morning and after a quick trip down to the Infirmary to get her hand checked, the girls joined the long queue to disembark. Just a short distance across the walkway and they were back on dry land, searching out their tour guide for the catamaran whale watching and beach trip.

They quickly found him holding up a lollipop sign with a number eight on it, and a couple of dozen or so of their fellow passengers crowded around. They waited another ten minutes for the stragglers and then they were off, walking down the embankment towards a gleaming white catamaran that awaited their arrival.

Four crew members busied themselves pouring drinks and preparing snacks as Donna and Fiona boarded the vessel and found some seats. Bob Marley blasted from the sound system, the morning sun already hot on their skin. Accepting a rum punch from one of the permanently smiling crew, Donna was finding it difficult to sit still as Bob belted out 'Buffalo Soldier'.

As soon as everyone was settled, the catamaran slowly made its way out of the harbour and headed out to sea.

"I presume he's the captain," said Fiona, as a young man began introducing the crew.

"Oh my word, he is beautiful," said Donna, gazing at the captain, his body moving to the music, dreadlocks blowing in the breeze.

"Donna!" exclaimed Fiona.

"No, I don't mean in that 'can't wait to rip his clothes off' kind of way. But look at that lovely face, so smiley and open, and a body that's just made to dance. He exudes life and happiness."

"How many of those rum punches have you downed?" asked Fiona.

"This is my first one. I'm pacing myself," Donna replied. Fiona laughed, fully aware that Donna had never paced herself at anything. "No, what I mean is that guy has got something extraordinary. He's so full of energy and vitality that you can't help but be drawn to him. Just look at all the female passengers."

"Yeah, I know what you mean," said Fiona, gazing around at all the women on board. The pure joy that exuded from the young man mesmerised them all. Even the men were enjoying his lively banter.

In a lilting Caribbean accent, he told them his name was Lionel; he was born and raised on the island and worked his socks off to buy his catamaran, his pride and joy. He said they had just heard over the radio that a pod of whales had been sighted and they were heading there now, although there was no guarantee they would still be there when they arrived.

Twenty minutes and another rum punch later, Donna felt the engines cut and the boat slowing.

"Look ahead and slightly to the left," pointed out one of the crew. "The whales are just under the surface, but will breach soon."

"How often do they breach?" asked the woman sitting next to Donna.

"It depends, but usually between seven to fifteen minutes, so you have to keep watching. We're not going any closer as we don't want to disturb them more than necessary."

"Are whales protected?" asked another passenger.

"Here in Dominica we have great respect for our wildlife and nature, and do our utmost to protect it. Our forestry, wildlife and parks are a division of our government and oversee the wellbeing of everything."

A collective cheer went up as a whale breached the surface and spouted air through its blowhole.

"It's a common misconception that the whales shoot water out through their blowholes," continued the guide. "It's actually warm air from the lungs, and as it meets the cooler air outside it condenses into a cloud, so to us it looks like a spray of water."

The questions and answers went on for a good thirty minutes as the whales continued to breach and splash back down into the water. It was a fantastic sight and seeing animals in their natural habitats was always a joy to Donna. It would be one of the beautiful memories the girls would take from their cruise.

Slowly the catamaran moved away from the pod, leaving them to their daily routine.

"OK," said Lionel, the effervescent captain, "we will leave the whales in peace now and head back towards the most perfect beach in the whole of the world. We'll stop for a while for a swim to cool off in the most perfect waters before we head closer to the beach, where the most perfect lunch and chill time await us this afternoon."

The girls laughed at his repetitive use of 'most perfect', but to Lionel everything in life was most perfect.

As the engines roared into life, Bob Marley reclaimed the airways, another round of rum punch was served, and the group settled back to chat and relax.

CHAPTER 42

William and Jenny wandered around the many shops and bars that littered the quayside, blissfully unaware that back in the UK they were being investigated by two amateur sleuths.

"Look at this," said Jason, turning his laptop around so Matt could read an old newspaper report he'd just found.

Husband Inherits Millions After Inconclusive Verdict

Dr William Mitchell, 28, of Hemmington, Berkshire, set to inherit nearly two million pounds after the inquest into his wife's death proved inconclusive.

"Bloody hell," exclaimed Matt. "Are you thinking he killed his wife to get her money?"

"It's a possibility, isn't it?"

"Yeah, it certainly is, and maybe he's done the same again with this wife. Where did wife number one get her money from?"

"Don't know," said Jason, "but I can check it out. Might be worth checking Eileen too, just to see if she had money in her own right."

"Does that report give any details on the death or the inquest?"

"No, not really. Think I would need to get the coroner's records to see the details."

"Can you do that?" asked Matt.

"It's a possibility. Might have to pay for it or call in a few favours, but I can try."

"I'm just checking through the births, deaths and marriages records so we can get some kind of timeline on this. I'm curious to see whether he had any children with the first wife."

"Good idea," said Jason, "a timeline can form the basis of our report back to Donna."

"I really miss those girls, you know," said Matt. "I worry about them when they're away."

"I miss them too. It amazes me how they manage to get themselves involved in so much trouble. I mean, a cruise should be easy and trouble free, shouldn't it?"

"You would think so, but not where those two are concerned."

"There's not much we can do though, just have to wait and see what happens next," said Jason.

"We could fly out and meet the ship at one of the islands it stops at," said Matt, wondering how possible that might be.

"I really don't think that will work," said Jason. "For one thing, what can we hope to achieve in such a short space of time? Secondly, what are the chances of us getting a cabin on board, and thirdly, there's the cost. We're not exactly rolling in money at the moment, are we?"

"True," replied Matt. "Perhaps we should consider opening a detective agency and charge for our services," he laughed as he got up to put the kettle on. He missed the thoughtful glint in Jason's eye.

Chapter 43

"Are you going in for a swim?" asked Fiona, as the catamaran came to a stop.

"You have got to be joking," Donna responded. "We're in the middle of the ocean, anything could be lurking down there."

"It's hardly the middle of the ocean, you can see the beach over there."

"Yeah, but my feet still won't touch the bottom. One of those whales could be waiting just beneath the surface."

"There are no whales here," said Lionel, laughing as he overheard the girls' conversation. "But if you want to get into the water we have life jackets, then your feet won't need to touch the bottom."

"Go on, Donna, have one then we can bob about in the ocean."

"Oh OK then, but woe betide you if this goes horribly wrong," she said, looking at Fiona.

Lionel went off in search of life jackets and Donna began to wonder if she had made the right decision. It's not that she didn't like being in water, but she never went out of her depth. Flashbacks of climbing down the ladder for their underwater walking trip in Malaysia sprang to mind. A trip that didn't end well.

"Here you go," said Lionel coming back with a couple of life jackets and helping Donna into one. "Do you need one too?" he asked Fiona.

"No thank you, I'm fine," she replied and caught sight of Donna mimicking her words, her head bobbing from side to side.

Lionel led them to the back of the catamaran and down the steps. He held onto Donna's hands as she slowly descended into the water and then gently released his grip. Donna was amazed that the life jacket kept her buoyant as she floated about in the ocean, waiting for Fiona to join her.

"This is really quite good, isn't it?" she said, with a grin on her face.

"Yes, it is. It's lovely to cool off from that intense heat."

Nearly everyone was in the water, a flotilla of bobbing heads enjoying the cool Caribbean Sea. The locals had been watching from the beach and as soon as the catamaran dropped anchor and discharged its passengers, they hastily filled their small vessels with handmade crafts and made their way towards the throng, trying to tempt the visitors to part with their money.

"That's all a bit pointless really," said Fiona. "None of us have any money with us, it's all on the boat."

"Perhaps they'll wait for you to go back and get some, you could always throw it overboard at them."

"Yeah and then they'll just paddle off with what we've bought."

"Oh Fi, you're so untrusting. Right, I'm heading back before I wrinkle completely."

"I'm coming too," Fiona replied, and they both slowly made their way to the back of the catamaran.

"Bloody hell, how on earth do I get my foot up there?" Donna exclaimed, looking at the bottom step level with her chest.

"Hold onto the rails and pull yourself up," suggested Fiona.

Try as she might, Donna could not haul herself up to the first step. She tried a hand on each rail, but as soon as she got her foot up to the step, she tipped over backwards. She tried both hands on the same rail, but that left her horizontal with no way of getting her head above her feet.

"Hold on," shouted Lionel, who could see the predicament she was in. "I'm coming in." He dived off the top step and into the water behind the girls.

"OK," he said, coming up behind Donna. "One hand on either side rail and bring your foot up to the step. Don't worry, you won't tip, I'm right behind you." Donna could feel his body on hers and his hands on her buttocks. "On the count of three, pull yourself up." He counted to three and as Donna pulled, he pushed and somehow between them she was standing on the first step. Luis, one of the crew, was on the second step waiting to take her hand and guide her back safely onto the deck.

"Right," said Lionel, turning to Fiona. "Your turn."

Both girls were relieved to be safely back on the boat.

"Bloody hell, Fi, I never thought getting back on would be that difficult. I had visions of being completely stranded at sea and washing up like a beached whale on the next island."

"Honestly, Donna, you do exaggerate. The crew would never let that happen; they wouldn't have a business if their passengers couldn't get back on."

The girls dried off and slipped back into their shorts and tops.

"Who's he?" asked Fiona, nodding towards a young man dressed all in black sitting at the front of the boat. "He wasn't here earlier."

Donna looked across at the man. A cold wave of fear washed over her.

Chapter 44

"Where are you going?" asked Fiona, as Donna left her seat.

"Need to find Lionel."

"I'll come with you."

"No," said Donna firmly. "Stay here and watch that man, but don't make it obvious."

"Why? What's the problem?"

"Tell you later, but please just do as I ask."

"Hello." Lionel was in the galley making up more rum punches. "You OK?"

"No, I'm not. There's a man sitting at the front of the boat and he wasn't there before we stopped for a swim. He's dressed in black trousers and a black jacket, which is odd in this heat. I have a very bad feeling about him." Donna put a hand on his arm as he walked towards the door, his face had lost its enchanting smile. "Don't make it obvious you're watching him."

"Take these," he said, handing her two plastic cups of punch. He picked up the tray of remaining drinks and together they left the galley. Donna walked back to her seat and handed a cup to Fiona.

"Donna, I really don't..."

"Just take it," Donna hissed. They were aware of Lionel sauntering towards the man at the front and offering him a drink. Taking the drink, he gulped it down in one go. Lionel saw why Donna was uneasy. The man was sweating, jumpy and nervous as he furtively glanced around at other passengers, never making eye contact.

With his eyes, Lionel beckoned Donna to follow.

"I'll take these back to the galley," she said, snatching Fiona's untouched drink and slowly sauntering away. Lionel already had the crew assembled in the cockpit by the time she arrived.

"I think the man in black has a bomb under his jacket. I'll radio ashore for help. Luis, you tell the passengers we have a slight problem with the engine but will be on our way soon. Donna, I don't want you or any of the passengers getting involved."

"I'm already involved, Lionel. That man out there," she said, pointing to the front of the catamaran, "is going to blow this boat and everyone on it to smithereens. We have got to stop him."

"How do we do that?" asked Sammy, the terrified youngest crew member.

"Luis, when you make the announcement, suggest the passengers might like to swim over to the shore where the beach bar will serve free drinks and snacks. Sammy, radio the bar and ask them to do just that. Tell Josie I'll pay her later. Shouldn't be a problem, I know the couple who run it. I want you all to get everyone off this boat as quickly as possible. I don't care how you do it, cajole, bribe, threaten if necessary, and then go with them."

"What do you want me to do?" asked Donna.

"Nothing, just get off the boat."

"Not going to happen," Donna replied, walking out of the cockpit.

Chapter 45

"What's going on, Don?" asked Fiona when Donna returned. "I need you to get off the boat."

"Why?"

"Because we think the man in black has a bomb under his jacket."

"Shit," said Fiona. "OK, let's go." She grabbed Donna's arm as she stood.

"No, not us," said Donna, pulling her arm back. "Just you."

"Don't be ridiculous," said Fiona. "I am not going anywhere without you."

Luis' announcement came over the sound system. A groan went up when the passengers heard there would be a delay because of engine trouble, but when they heard mention of free drinks and snacks at the beach bar, they soon stripped down to their swimwear and headed back into the water.

Donna walked to the back of the boat, followed by Fiona. They were unseen by the man in black.

"Here, take this." Donna strapped a waterproof bum-bag around Fiona's waist.

"Donna, what the bloody hell are you playing at?"

"Fiona, I need you off this boat now."

"And I'm telling you, I am not going without you."

"Oh yes you bloody well are." Donna gave Fiona an almighty push and in an instant she was over the side and bobbing about in the water.

Donna walked back to the man in black and sat by his side. She felt the energy coming off him in waves, smothering her like a dark descending cloud. She wanted nothing more than to move away, get off the boat as fast as she could. But she couldn't. She knew she needed to at least try to talk to him, to connect in some way, to try to save him and also Lionel's beloved catamaran.

"You not going ashore while we wait for the engine to be fixed?" she asked him.

"No."

"I'm Donna, by the way. What's your name?"

He ignored her.

"Get off the boat now, Donna, you can't save him." She heard Angelo's voice clearly.

She ignored him.

"I'm here with my best friend Fiona," Donna carried on. "We go on holiday every year together. We met at university many, many years ago." Donna knew she was rambling, but wanted to keep him distracted until help arrived. "It's so beautiful here, isn't it?"

"I don't want to be here," he said suddenly.

"You can leave. You can go to the beach with the others."

"I mean in this world, I don't want to be in this world."

"Well, that's your choice to make, but it seems an awful waste to me."

"Why do you say that? You don't even know me."

"No, I've never met you before, and I don't even know your name, but I know *you*." Donna felt way out of her depth, she was trying to keep calm and talk a suicide bomber out of blowing himself up. She had no idea what to say. *Angelo, if ever I needed your help it's now,* she thought. *Give me the words to say.* She heard his voice in her head – *let it flow from the heart.*

"Daniel, I think I'll call you Daniel if that's OK. Daniel, my love, I can't begin to understand how you're feeling right now, and I know nothing about what's brought you here and to this decision. But I can feel your pain and anguish. I care, Daniel. I care what happens to you and to throw it away because today is the worst day ever seems such a waste."

He looked at her then, really looked at her, unsure whether they were just words or if she meant them. Donna felt she had made a connection.

"Daniel, one thing I learnt when life got tough for me and I felt like I had hit rock bottom, is that the only way is up. Things never stay the same forever. The sun will shine again. It may not be tomorrow, but it will shine."

"Easy for you to say."

"Yes, it is now, but there was a time when I didn't think the sun would ever shine again, but I just took it one day at a time. So live in the moment. Enjoy now, sitting here on this beautiful boat in the warm sunshine, two friends having a chat. Don't think about how crap your life is, just enjoy now."

"You're the only person who's ever bothered to talk to me. I mean really talk. You somehow know exactly what I'm feeling. You're a very special person."

***

In the beach bar the holidaymakers were singing, dancing and enjoying the free beverages, curtesy of the catamaran crew. Only Fiona remained standing on the beach, looking towards the boat. She desperately wanted to go back and find Donna. What on earth had possessed her friend to push her overboard? They were a team, for God's sake, they should be in this together.

Luis watched her from the veranda. Concerned that she might try to make it back to the boat, he wandered out and stood by her side.

"You OK?" he asked.

"No, not really. Donna pushed me off the boat and I should be there with her. God knows what's happening."

"The coastguard and the police are on their way out there now. Look, you can just about see them approaching from the blind side. I doubt that Donna and that crazy halfwit will even know they're there."

They saw plumes of black smoke and flames rising into the air, a second or two before they heard the explosion.

Chapter 46

"Look at this," said Jason, picking up a sheet of paper off the printer and pushing it towards Matt.

"What is it?"

"It's the coroner's summary on the first wife."

Matt quickly read through the document. It was brief, but to the point.

"So basically it's saying that the cause of death was inconclusive. They could find no anomalies other than a higher than normal level of potassium chloride in her system."

"Yeah. That triggers alarm bells, doesn't it?"

"Certainly does," replied Matt. "I've googled Eileen and the first wife and they both inherited substantial amounts of money from their families. Eileen's father was a wealthy farmer and landowner, and when he died, she sold the estate for millions. I'm presuming that will now go to William."

"Jeez," Jason whistled. "He certainly knows how to choose his women, doesn't he?"

"Might be worth checking the secretary out and see how she compares."

"Mmm," murmured Jason. "If she has money, then I think we've hit gold. I'll do a quick search, do you have her name?"

"Yeah," replied Matt, looking through his notebook. "It's Jenny Jones, so might take a while to find the right one. I've put together a timeline, so think we're almost ready to send it to the girls. Let's hope it's good enough for the security guy to take it seriously."

"Anything strike you as odd?" asked Jason.

"Well yeah, William was married to his first wife for just a year, they had no children. He married Eileen just three months after wife number one died. Now that's quick and I have to wonder whether he had her on standby."

"Possible. Let's draw up a list of questions we would ask William if we had the chance. Might be helpful to the girls."

"Right," replied Matt. "I'd like to know whether he was having an affair with Eileen before his first wife died."

Jason created a new document on his laptop and headed it 'Questions for William'.

"Question number one – was he having an affair with Eileen before his first wife died?"

"Question number two – why did he marry Eileen so quickly?"

"Question number three – did William know that his first wife was a wealthy woman?"

"Question number four – did he know Eileen had money?"

The questions continued to flow and after half an hour or so, they had a list of over twenty. There would be many more, depending on the answers William gave.

Another hour passed, each of them absorbed in their work.

"I've found her," said Jason, sitting back in his chair and running his fingers through his hair.

"Well done, sugar," said Matt. "Your ability to investigate is paying off."

"It's all pretty routine stuff to be honest. Jenny certainly doesn't have the kind of money that the two wives had, but she inherited a few grand and a property when her mother died last year."

"Interesting," said Matt. "Does it say how much, or whether she sold the property? She might have to share that with siblings of course."

"Doesn't say," replied Jason. "I need to do a lot more work before I have the answers."

"Right, I'll just finish this off and send it over to Donna, then shall we go to the pub to eat? Don't think I can be bothered to cook."

"Good idea," Jason smiled. "Shall we ask Dave?"

"Yeah. Can't be much fun being on his own now the boys are doing their own thing."

"I'll WhatsApp him, but don't mention what the girls have got themselves into now. Donna doesn't want him to know."

"That's a big mistake," Jason grinned.

"It sure is."

Chapter 47

The beach bar emptied immediately, locals joining customers lining the beach, looking on in total disbelief. The wreckage slowly drifted out of the smoke, moving across the bay.

Fiona fell to her knees, a low keening gathering strength as her whole body began to shake. Luis dropped beside her and pulled her into his arms.

"I need to find Donna." Pulling away suddenly, she stood and ran down to the water's edge. "Donna!" she screamed at the top of her voice. She didn't stop running until the depth of the ocean slowed her down. Luis was right behind her.

"No, you can't go," he said, trying to pull her back.

"I have to."

She wrenched her arm away from him with such force they both fell into the water. She picked herself up, resuming her journey out to the wreckage.

"Donna!" she continued to scream, her voice becoming hoarse.

A couple more men joined Luis and between them they pulled Fiona back to the beach. Her strength was waning as grief took over. She sobbed into the arms of one of her fellow passengers.

"What the fuck has just happened?" asked another passenger.

"A man got on board when we finished our swim, he must have come from one of the canoes selling stuff," Luis began to explain. "We believe he had a bomb."

"Oh my God," said one woman, holding her face in her hands. "Was everyone off the boat?"

"No, sadly not. Fiona's friend Donna was still on board, as was Lionel, the owner. Please take care of her," he nodded towards Fiona. "There are things I need to do." He ran over to where Josie and her husband were standing, mouthed something, and the three disappeared inside the bar.

Thirty minutes later, he rejoined the others on the beach. Everyone crowded around, eager to hear what he had to say.

"I'm sorry, but I have no real news. The coastguards have confirmed that they received a mayday call from the catamaran, and they have despatched a boat to the scene. They await further news and details."

"Are there any bodies?" asked a passenger.

"They don't know I'm afraid," responded Luis. "A bus is on its way to take you all back to your ship."

"What about our things that we left on the boat?" asked a young woman at the back of the group. "My bag had my phone in it, as well as other stuff."

"I'm sure there will be a recovery operation of some sort, and anything that is salvaged will hopefully be returned to you. But I can't tell you when that will be or how long it will take. We should have more news soon."

"I hope there'll be compensation, my phone was top-of-the-range and very expensive," the woman continued.

"I'm sure that phones and bags are the last thing on any of our minds when there are lives at stake," an older lady retorted.

The young woman gave a disdainful look and was just about to give a retort when her husband placed a warning hand on her shoulder.

"Not now, love, emotions are riding high as it is without you causing a scene."

"The bus has just arrived," Luis informed them, "so please make your way across. The coastguard will inform your ship of news and updates.

"Come on, love, let's get you on the bus," said Diane, a fellow passenger. Her husband, Roy, helped Fiona to her feet and slowly led her across the sand towards the bus.

"I can't go without Donna," she cried.

"You have to, darling," said Diane. "When there's news I'm sure we'll all be told, but we need to be back on the ship to hear it. In the meantime, we're both here for you."

Chapter 48

A small party of crew members was waiting for the bus when it arrived back in port. The passengers all needed debriefing, some more so than others, and one of the smaller bars on board had been closed to other guests for the afternoon.

Susanne greeted everyone as they climbed the walkway and Julien, one of the junior officers, led them to the bar.

"Would anyone like a drink?" Julien asked. "Please feel free to order anything you want, there's no charge."

Diane led Fiona over to a table and helped her into a chair. Fiona had been in a catatonic-like state ever since the bomb exploded.

"Get her a brandy, Roy," Diane said to her husband, "and I'll have one too."

"Hello, how are you both doing?" asked Susanne. It was her job to assess how well the guests were coping with the traumatic event they had witnessed and whether they needed any further help.

"Fiona here is not doing too good," Diane explained. "Her friend was on the catamaran when it exploded."

"OK," said Susanne, looking closely at Fiona. "It looks as if she's in shock. I'll get the medics to see her. Please don't let her leave here before she's been seen."

"What's happening?" asked Roy, returning to the table with three brandies.

"She's going to get the medics to check Fiona. She's probably in shock, poor love."

Ten minutes later the captain strode into the bar and picked up the microphone.

"Ladies and gentlemen, first of all I am deeply shocked and saddened by today's events, and I can't begin to imagine how you must all be feeling. Rest assured that we are doing all that we can to help you cope with the situation and we have trained staff ready to assist. I have spoken to the coastguard and, unfortunately, they have very little information at this time.

After the distress call was received, a police vessel was immediately dispatched to the area. We understand that three individuals were still on the catamaran just before the explosion, but it is unclear whether or not they are alive. A full-scale investigation will now take place. That's all the information I have at this time but please rest assured you will all be kept informed. If you have any questions, please ask one of the crew. Thank you."

"What about our stuff?" asked the young woman who was more concerned with her phone.

"As many items as possible will be salvaged from the wreckage and returned to their owners," replied the captain, before making his way out of the bar.

"Hello, Fiona, I'm the medical officer on board but I believe we're already met." Fiona turned her head and looked at him with vacant eyes.

"Brandy?" the medic asked Roy, pointing to the glass. Roy nodded. "Fiona, can you take a tiny little sip of this please?" he coaxed, lifting the goblet to her lips. The alcohol made her cough and splutter as she quickly snapped back into awareness.

"That's better," said the medic, picking up her hand and feeling for her pulse.

"Donna?" she asked, hope springing to her face.

"There's no news yet I'm afraid. Now, Fiona, I need you to tell me exactly what happened."

Slowly Fiona started to talk. They took several breaks, allowing her to cry and blow her nose, but bit by bit the story came out.

"Why is he making her relive all this?" Diane asked Susanne. "It all seems a bit cruel."

"Believe me, it's best that she starts to talk about her experience as soon as possible. Keeping everything bottled up is unhealthy and can lead to problems further down the line."

An hour later and the medical officer was satisfied with progress. Fiona had been given a cup of tea, a couple of biscuits and had finished her brandy. Her face had regained some of its colour and she was alert and talking.

"I'm going to give you something to help you sleep, Fiona, and I suggest you now go back to your cabin and get some rest."

"No, not yet. I want to wait a bit longer in case there's any more news."

"OK, but promise me you will take these when you go to bed. You need to rest both your mind and body." Fiona nodded meekly.

Some guests started to wander away, leaving just a handful in the bar.

"Diane, Roy, why don't you both go. It's nearly time for dinner and you must be starving. Thank you so much for your help, I don't know what I would have done without you both."

"No, we won't go and leave you," said Diane, still concerned for Fiona's well-being.

"Honestly, you go," Fiona urged, as she saw Carol and Jess coming through the doors and searching for her. "I'll be fine now."

Chapter 49

Dinner was a rather subdued affair without the four women. It was they who really brought the group together, with their endless chatter and infectious laughter. Alan and Sue really missed them, and Win was becoming bored with William's self-inflated ego.

"I wonder why the girls are not here tonight?" Sue said.

"Probably gone off to some posh restaurant," grunted William, always miffed that someone might be getting something better than him.

"Well, I for one miss them," said Win. "I hope they're back tomorrow."

"Frederick," Sue called to their waiter. "Do you know where the girls are tonight? It's so quiet without them."

"I don't know for sure," Frederick replied, "but I heard that there was some sort of incident on one of the trips. Maybe they got caught up in that."

"What kind of incident?" asked William. All eyes turned to Frederick, waiting for his reply.

"All I know is that one of the catamarans exploded and somebody is missing."

"Well, well, well," started William, before Sue cut him short.

"Oh my word," exclaimed Sue. "I hope it's not one of our girls."

William was in quite a good mood as he and Jenny left the dining room and wandered off to their favourite bar.

"What do you make of this catamaran exploding?" asked Jenny, as they settled into a couple of comfy chairs, enjoying their after-dinner brandies. "Do you think it might involve the ladies?"

"I have no idea, Jenny, but at least it's taken the heat off us."

"What do you mean?"

"The four of them have developed an unhealthy interest in our affairs since Eileen died. You've already noticed their endless questions, which is surprising because I'm not sure you really listen to the dinner conversation. If one of them has gone missing, it's one less to worry about."

Chapter 50

Dave sent a quick reply back to Matt – 'grabbing a quick shower, meet you down the pub'.

"Right, let's go," Matt said, collecting his wallet and keys from the kitchen worktop. "Dave will meet us there."

As they walked out of Angel Crescent, Jason turned and looked back at the five houses.

"This is such a wonderful place to live," he said. "I'll be heartbroken when Tom comes home and we have to leave."

"Me too, sugar, me too. But that's a way off yet and anything can happen between now and then."

"It's a shame Dave didn't build six houses. Wonder if there's space to squeeze another one in."

"A shed in the garden would do me," laughed Jason.

The pub was fairly crowded when they arrived. Matt went in search of a table whilst Jason chatted amicably with the barmaid as she poured three pints of lager. Grateful to be accepted as one of the locals so quickly, he waved across the bar to Bob, who ran the village shop.

"You know I'm not entirely happy with Donna not letting Dave know what's going on," Jason said, placing the glasses down on the beer mats scattered around the table. "It's even harder when we know and are working with her."

"I know what you mean," replied Matt. "I hate keeping secrets. He'll find out, and then we'll be blamed for not telling him. He definitely won't want to let Donna out of his sight again, and that will cause more arguments."

"He's sure to want to talk about the girls tonight."

"I think we ought to tell him what's going on. After all, he's our friend too."

"I agree," Jason said, taking a swig of lager.

Dave entered the bar and looked around for his two friends. He spotted Matt at the corner table and made his way over.

"Hi guys," he said, pulling out a chair. "Are we celebrating something?"

"No," laughed Jason. "We've been working all day and neither of us could be bothered to cook."

"Great idea, saves me cooking too. What have you been working on?" He looked quizzically from Matt to Jason, then back at Matt, neither of them keen to answer his question.

"What's going on?" he asked.

"I've had a message from Donna," Matt told him. "It's nothing to worry about and they're both fine, but one of the passengers has died and they're suspicious of the husband so she asked us to check him out."

"Oh for God's sake, why can't the pair of them just mind their own business?"

"Because that's not who they are, Dave," Jason chipped in. "For some strange reason they want to right all wrongs in the world and if they feel that someone is being treated unfairly, they just have to help."

"That's a noble thing, but it puts them in all sorts of danger, as we've already seen."

"Yes it does," said Matt, "but they should be safe on a cruise ship."

"I hope you're right, but looking at their past exploits I wouldn't be too sure. I won't rest until the pair of them are back home."

"I think that goes for all of us," said Matt, picking up their empty glasses and heading towards the bar.

Chapter 51

Fiona awoke from her drug induced sleep early the next morning. For just the briefest of moments she thought Donna was in the bathroom and all was well in her world. Then she remembered. She turned quickly, hoping to see her friend lying in the other bed next to her, but it was empty and hadn't been slept in. Donna was missing, presumed dead. A fresh wave of tears tracked down her already blotched and puffy face.

The ship had set sail the previous evening, unable to remain in the port of Dominica any longer. Fiona didn't want to leave. How could she possibly leave the last place she had been with Donna? It was unthinkable. But Diane and Roy had brought her back safely and the staff were doing their best to look after her.

She couldn't face a day without her best friend by her side. How on earth would she explain it to Dave? She needed to tell Matt and Jason. How would Donna's boys cope without their mum? *Oh Donna, why the hell didn't you get off the boat with me?*

A soft knocking on her cabin door roused her from her thoughts. Bernard, their cabin steward, used his own key and quietly let himself in. He called to her softly.

"Good morning, ma'am, I've brought you some breakfast."

"No, I don't want it. Please take it away, Bernard, but thank you."

"Ma'am, you have to eat, you have to keep your strength up."

"Why? What do I need my strength for?"

"Because you must never give up hope." Bernard left the tray on the table and quietly left the cabin. He hoped she would at least drink some of the tea.

Oh Angelo, where are you? she thought as she sank back down in the bed. Her thoughts were on a continuous loop running through her mind. *I hope you're there because Donna and I need you right now. Where is she, Angelo? Is she safe? Is she still alive? Please bring her back to me. Angelo, I've never asked you for anything before, but I'm begging you now, please bring Donna back.*

An hour later she was still lying in bed, her breakfast untouched. She couldn't sleep, she couldn't get up either. She felt paralysed with fear and a grief so deep that she had never felt before. Even losing Nikos hadn't affected her the way losing Donna had. She didn't know what to do, she didn't know how to function.

A sharp rap on her cabin door brought her back to the present.

"Bernard, I don't want anything. Please just leave me alone," she called as she heard the door open.

"Fiona, it's Susanne," came the voice. Fiona flew out of bed.

"Is there news?" she asked, hope making her heart beat a little faster.

"Yes, but don't get your hopes up just yet. We've just heard from the coastguard in Dominica that two people have been pulled from the water and taken to the local hospital. We don't know who, or their medical condition, but will hear as soon as they have more news, which hopefully won't be too much longer."

"Oh my God, she's alive?" Fiona brought her hands to her face, her eyes wide with renewed hope.

"Don't get too excited, Fiona, we don't have any details as yet. But rest assured, as soon as we have an update you will be told."

Chapter 52

Matt had emailed his report to Donna when they got back from the pub, and was surprised he'd not heard from her that morning. Maybe there was nothing to say, he reasoned. Or maybe she hadn't read it yet. He checked the time difference, and yes it was a possibility. But something nagged at him.

"I've not heard back from the girls yet, do you think they're OK?" he asked Jason as he walked into the kitchen to refill his coffee cup.

"I'm sure they're fine," Jason replied, hoping that Matt was fretting about nothing. "You know what those two are like when they're having fun."

"Mmm, I suppose you're right. Maybe I'll just try giving her a call."

"Sweetheart, it's the middle of the night where they are so she won't thank you for waking her up. That's if she's not put her phone on silent of course. You just have to be patient and wait until she gets back to you."

"I suppose so but I'm going to be on tenterhooks until I hear back from her. God, I'm sounding more like Dave every day."

"That's not a bad thing," Jason smiled, "shows you care."

Lunchtime came and went, and he'd still heard nothing. He'd sent three more emails since breakfast, each unread.

"Jason, she's not reading the emails I've sent." Matt wandered into the garden, phone in hand, and scrolling up and down. Jason let out a sigh. Sitting under the shade of their big umbrella, he was trying to write a story, but it was not going well.

He was trying to build his name and business as a freelance investigative journalist by writing stories and exposés and selling them to newspapers and magazines. He'd had a little success but needed to up the ante if he was to make a good living at it. He was seriously considering starting his own blog site and adding in some podcasts. Matt's whittling on about the girls was hindering his concentration.

"How do you know she's not reading them?"

"Because I put a mark when read thingy on all my emails so people can't say they never received one from me."

"But that can be overridden."

"But this is Donna, she wouldn't think to do that."

"What's the time in Dominica now?" he asked, turning to face Matt and giving him his full attention.

"Twenty past nine in the morning," replied Matt, checking his watch.

"They're probably still sleeping off the night before. Wait until this evening before you start getting too anxious."

Matt turned and walked back inside the house, leaving Jason alone to get on with his story. He wondered if he should talk to Dave. He saw him leave for work that morning but didn't know whether he'd returned. He poked his head out of the front door, checking to see whether the van was back. It wasn't.

He rummaged through the freezer trying to find something for dinner that evening, not that he felt like eating. He wished he could shake the feeling of impending doom. *Blimey*, he thought, *I'm becoming more like Donna with these feelings.*

The afternoon dragged on. He sent another couple of emails. No reply. He googled the ship and the itinerary and idly pondered the possibility of flying out to the next port of call. They were due in St Lucia the following morning. He checked flights into Hewanorra International Airport.

"Do you want a beer?" asked Jason, walking into the kitchen.

"Yeah," he replied absentmindedly.

"Still nothing from the girls?" Jason asked.

"Nope."

"OK then, why don't we wait till the morning and if still nothing, we'll see if we can get a flight out."

"Agreed, think that's the best thing we can do."

"Yes, but I'm sure you'll hear something before then."

Chapter 53

As soon as Susanne left the cabin, Fiona went into the bathroom. Filled with renewed hope, she took a shower and dressed. She wanted to be ready when the news came.

By mid-morning Fiona was losing patience. She needed to know where her friend was. She tried reading her book to while away the hours but she couldn't concentrate. She paced around the cabin, tidying away the things that Donna had left strewn around.

Her thoughts were see-sawing, one minute she was sure that Donna had survived, then she didn't feel so sure. What if she's been badly injured, what if her limbs had been blown off in the explosion. God, her mind was really feeding her worse case scenarios.

Bernard came back to make the beds and clean the cabin.

"No news yet?" he asked.

"No," she replied. "They've pulled two people from the water but I don't know whether they are alive or dead, and I don't know who they are."

"That's possibly a good sign," said Bernard, hoping upon hope that he was right. "At least there's still hope."

Fiona nodded her head, an absent look on her face. She'd drifted off into her own world, where her thoughts took centre stage. She wasn't sure how much more she could take.

Silently Bernard left the cabin. There was nothing he could say to provide comfort.

An hour later and Susanne knocked on the door.

"Fiona," she called, "can I come in?"

Fiona quickly rose out of her seat and all but pulled Susanne into the cabin, an eager and expectant look on her face.

"Fiona," she began, as she moved her across to the sofa and gently took her hand. "I don't want you to get your hopes up, but the coastguard has just confirmed that they have pulled two people from the water, and they have been taken to hospital. They have no further information at the moment but are in contact with the local police and will pass on our details. The police will let us know as soon as they have more information."

"They're alive?" whispered Fiona, needing to ask but afraid of the answer.

"Yes," Susanne replied.

Fiona began to cry, relief and optimism spreading through her once again.

"Fiona, have you eaten today?"

"No, but I don't want anything," she replied, shaking her head.

"You have to eat," Susanne said, quickly contacting room service. She remained with Fiona until the quick knock on the door heralded the arrival of refreshments. Susanne let the waiter in and was surprised to see one of the guests directly behind him.

"Hello, I'm Carol, one of Fiona's dinner companions and now friend. Can I see her?"

"Fiona," called Susanne, "is it OK if Carol comes in?"

"Yes, of course." Fiona stood as Carol came towards her.

"Any news?" asked Carol, pulling Fiona in for a hug.

"I'll leave you two to it," said Susanne. "Can you make sure she eats something?" she asked as she passed Carol.

Fiona told Carol the latest update.

"So there's still hope," said Carol. Fiona simply nodded.

"Here," she said, "eat a couple of these." Carol pulled cling film off a plate of various sandwiches and held them out to Fiona. The smell of food filled the air and Fiona's stomach gave a rumble.

"No, thank you. I don't want anything to eat."

"Eat one please," Carol said firmly. "You need to keep your strength up. Just take one."

Fiona plucked a sandwich from the plate and took a small bite, totally unaware of what she was eating. When she finished the first, Carol got her to take a second quarter, feeling happier that Fiona at last had something in her stomach.

In less than an hour Susanne was back.

Chapter 54

"Fiona," she called, as Carol opened the door and beckoned her inside. "Donna is alive and well." Fiona stared at her, wide-eyed. She watched the tears flow slowly down Fiona's cheeks, feeling her emotion and eyes starting to brim.

Carol stood next to her, an arm around her shoulders.

"I don't know the full story," she continued, "but no doubt Donna will fill us in when she gets back. It seems a young man boarded the catamaran with a bomb strapped to his body. How Donna knew what was going to happen is unclear, but she told the captain of the catamaran, who immediately called the coastguard."

"Angelo," whispered Fiona.

"Sorry?" said Susanne.

"Angelo, he told her about the bomb."

"I'm sorry, I don't understand. Who's Angelo?"

"Never mind."

"Well anyway, they pulled Donna and the captain off the vessel seconds before it exploded. Both were taken to the local hospital and kept overnight. They have been discharged this morning and Donna will be flown to St Lucia, ready to rejoin the ship when we dock in the morning."

"Umm... I er... it's..." Fiona stumbled over her words, not really knowing what she wanted to say.

"Don't say anything now. This has all been a tremendous shock for you. You need to process and try to make sense of everything first. There is nothing more you can do, Fiona, so try to relax knowing your friend is alive and well. I'll get one of the medical team to pop in and check on you, and food will be delivered. Make sure you eat. We'll talk again tomorrow."

"Thank you," Fiona whispered, as Susanne left the cabin.

Chapter 55

Donna opened her eyes and a moment of panic set in. She didn't know where she was, or how she had got there. She moved nothing but her eyes, slowly looking around the room.

She was in a hospital, with a drip in the back of her hand.

"What the fuck?" she thought.

Then she remembered.

She was on the catamaran and had sat next to the man in black, the one with the bomb. She started talking in a chatty, friendly way. She remembered Angelo telling her to get off the boat, that she couldn't save him. She took no notice and carried on talking. The bomber slowly started to listen and respond to her. She felt she had made a connection.

Suddenly there was a quick jerk from behind and she tumbled backwards and into the water. Arms held her tightly as they sank lower and lower into the depths of the ocean. She couldn't breathe, panic set in. She started flailing her arms and legs.

A mask came from behind and was placed over her face.

"Breathe," a voice said. She wasn't sure whether she heard it or whether it was in her head. 'Angelo?' she thought. She gulped in air. Then the mask was gone. She held her breath, trying desperately not to panic. She kicked her legs and flailed her arms. The mask came back again.

"Breathe," the voice said.

Slowly they rose and as she broke the surface of the water, she gulped in clean, fresh air.

Strong arms turned her onto her back and pulled her towards a waiting vessel. More strong arms pulled her on board and laid her gently on the floor, a blanket was placed around her. Totally bewildered, she was vaguely aware of another body being hauled onto the small vessel and then they were speeding towards the shore. An ambulance waited. She must have drifted off to sleep then because she couldn't remember much after that.

A doctor walked towards her.

"Ahh good, you are awake now. How do you feel?"

"Apart from a bit of a headache, I'm OK. But more importantly, where am I and what happened?"

"You are in the local hospital. You came in yesterday, totally confused and in shock. You had no physical injuries, so we have just given you fluids and a mild sedative. As to what happened, I will leave that to the police to bring you up to date."

"I need to get back to the ship. Where's Fiona? Can I leave?"

"Yes, I am happy for you to leave, and I believe arrangements are being made to get you back. I know the police are in contact with your ship. Take things easy for a few days and get plenty of rest."

"Fiona?"

"I believe all passengers are safely back on board."

As the doctor left, two police officers walked in.

"Good morning, how are you feeling?" one of them asked.

"I'm fine. What happened?"

"We need to take a statement from you, but it appears that one of the coastguards pulled you from the front of the catamaran just before the bomb detonated and the vessel exploded."

"Oh my God," Donna exclaimed. "Did Daniel trigger it on purpose?"

"Daniel, was that the bomber's name?" the second officer asked.

"I've no idea, it's just what I called him. He was quite sweet really, but in a really dark place. I think I might have been able to talk him round." Donna put her head down, deeply sad that she hadn't had the chance to save him.

"Lionel?" she suddenly asked. "What happened to Lionel?"

"He's fine. He jumped just before the cat blew." Donna breathed a sigh of relief.

"Just Daniel who died then?"

"Yes. Which is just as it should be. He put lives in danger on a selfish whim." Donna took a different view.

Chapter 56

Fiona was first down the walkway as soon as the ship docked the following morning and everything was secured. She stood waiting patiently for her friend to arrive. One of the staff brought her a chair and insisted she sit in the shade, under the awning being set up in readiness to hand out refreshing drinks to the hot and tired passengers returning later in the day.

"Why don't you wait on board?" asked Steve, another kind and caring crew member. "It's much cooler inside, and more comfortable."

"No, I'm fine honestly. Once Donna gets on board there's no knowing where she will go and I don't want to miss her."

"Is she the one who got caught up in that catamaran explosion?" he asked.

"Yes."

"She's lucky to be alive. One of my colleagues, and a good friend, flew across to Dominica to escort her back. I'm sure they'll be here as soon as they can."

Fiona settled down to read her book. She brought it with her to while away the time, but she couldn't settle. Every time she heard a vehicle approach, her head shot up. Most were trucks bringing supplies, and tour buses taking passengers out on their trips.

"Fiona! Fiona!" shouted Steve, a couple of hours later. "They're here."

Fiona stood and ran towards the taxi as it pulled up as close to the gate as it could. She watched as a female officer climbed out of the near side, and then she saw Donna's head bobbing at the far side.

"Donna!" she yelled, waving her arms in the air.

"Fiona," Donna called back, running towards her best friend. The pair hugged and cried and hugged some more, both totally relieved that all was well and Donna was back safe and sound.

"Now that was a scene worthy of any film," laughed Steve, as they made their way towards the gangway.

"I suppose we'd better get back to the cabin so you can have a rest," said Fiona, her arm still entwined with Donna's.

"Sod that," said Donna, "let's hit a bar, I need a drink."

Chapter 57

After a couple of drinks and a bite to eat, Fiona finally persuaded Donna to go back to the cabin for a rest.

"Donna, it's been a tough couple of days for both of us and this euphoric state that we're both in now that it's all over will wear off soon. We need to be relaxed and in a good place when we come back down to earth."

"OK, I hear you," said Donna, draining the last of the wine from her glass. "Let's go."

Back in the cabin, Donna pulled her phone from the bedside drawer.

"Bugger, battery's dead," she said, rooting around for the charging cable. "I need to see if there's an email from Matt."

"Tell me what happened, Don," said Fiona gently.

"You know what happened."

"No, I don't. I know the rough outline, but I need you to tell me what actually happened to you." Fiona knew it was important for Donna to talk, to share the trauma to lessen its impact.

Donna gave a deep sigh and sat silently for a while.

"Someone pulled me off the catamaran, it exploded, I ended up in hospital but I'm OK and back with you now. That's it."

"No, love, that's not it," Fiona said quietly. "Start from when we noticed the man in black."

Donna sighed again. She really didn't want to do this right now, but knew that Fiona was forcing the issue for her own good.

"As soon as you pointed out the man in black I knew that something was seriously wrong and that something big was about to happen. I found Lionel and told him of my fears and he didn't argue. He called the coastguard and the rest of crew started to get everyone off the cat. I knew you would be my biggest problem, I had to push you off to keep you safe. Lionel urged me to leave too, but I knew I had to try and stop the bomber.

"I went to the front of the cat and sat talking to him. After a while he started responding. I called him Daniel. He was in a very dark place, and he could see no way out. He said I was the only one who ever really listened to him, who understood.

"I heard Angelo tell me to get off the boat, that I couldn't save him, but I took no notice. I thought I was talking him round, Fi. I thought I could make a difference to that young man's life." Donna stopped talking for a couple of minutes. Fiona kept quiet, knowing she would start talking again soon.

"Hands came from behind and pulled me backwards into the water. I kept going down, deeper and deeper. I couldn't breathe, I thought I was going to die. Arms came around my body and a mask was placed over my face. Someone said breathe. Maybe it was Angelo. I got some air and then the mask was gone. The mask kept coming and going. Eventually we broke through the surface and I was put in an ambulance.

"The next thing I knew was waking up in hospital. The doctor told me I was fine, no physical injuries, just shock. They told me that as I was pulled from the cat, the bomb exploded. I guess we'll never know whether it was an accident or whether Daniel triggered it.

"Anyway, they discharged me from the hospital and a lovely crew member met me. We flew here to St Lucia, spent the night in a hotel until we could rejoin the ship this morning. And that's just about it."

"Why did you ignore Angelo, why didn't you just get off the boat?"

"Because I really thought I could save him. I know Angelo won't be happy with me, but I couldn't just abandon Daniel. We all have free will, and I just had to try and help. Anyway, Angelo saved me in the end."

"Oh Donna, what am I going to do with you?" Fiona moved across to Donna's bed and gave her friend a big hug. She loved her dearly for her kindness to others, but she was exasperated by her at times too.

"Right, phone's got enough life in it now. Thank God I popped it into the bag before strapping it round your waist, otherwise we would have lost everything. I just need to check to see if there's anything from Matt and Jason."

Chapter 58

"Oh God, there's half a dozen messages from Matt," said Donna as her phone sprang to life and she connected to the ship's Wi-Fi.

"You'd better answer him before they send out the flying squad or such like," laughed Fiona.

Hi Matt

All good with us, no need to panic. Ship's Wi-Fi is a bit hit and miss. Will delve into your emails shortly.

Love D xx

"There, that should keep them all quiet for a while. I hope he hasn't worried Dave with all his nonsense."

"It's not nonsense though, is it, Don? They all seriously worry about us when we go off somewhere, and let's face it, they have good reason to."

"Yes, you're right. If Dave knew about this latest escapade he'd never let me out of his sight again."

"Can't really blame him, can you?"

"S'pose not. Right, let's see what Matt and Jason's report says." Donna opened the first email from Matt and downloaded the attachment. "Oh my God," she exclaimed as she read through the document. "Look at this," she said, passing her phone to Fiona.

Matt got straight to the point in his report and had drawn up a comprehensive timeline.

1950 – William Mitchell born, father a GP, mother housewife

1976 – William married Ruth Connelly, daughter of a wealthy landowner and farmer

1978 – Ruth dies and William inherits roughly £2m

1978 – William marries Eileen Cousins

1981 – William buys GP practice

1982 – Son Malcolm born

1987 – Daughter Sarah born

2015 – William retires from practice, son takes over

That's the timeline for now, but we are still investigating. However, you might like to know that the inquest into the first wife's death was inconclusive, so death recorded as natural causes. Jason is trying to get the full coroner's report.

Eileen was the only child of a very wealthy farmer and landowner, and she inherited everything when her parents died. Again, we're still investigating, but it looks like William is set to inherit the lot.

William certainly rings alarm bells for me and is definitely worth pursuing. Will keep digging and let you have updates when we get them.

Love M&J xx

"Bloody hell," Fiona exclaimed. "Looks like we're on the right track then?"

"Yeah it does. Need to chat with Carol and Jess and then decide where we go from here. Right, I'm off to the bathroom for a long, hot shower."

Chapter 59

The look on William's and Jenny's faces when Fiona and Donna joined the table for dinner was a picture. It was clear that neither one of them expected to see the girls again.

"It's so good to have you both back," said Sue, jumping from her seat to give them a hug.

"It certainly is," said Alan, standing behind his wife, with Win waiting patiently behind him.

"Missed you both," said Carol quietly as she and Jess formed a hug circle with Donna and Fiona.

"Gin Bar later?" asked Donna.

"You bet," said Jess.

"Ladies," exclaimed Frederick, moving towards the table with a hand on his heart. "My day is complete now you are both back."

"Oh Frederick, you are such a charmer," laughed Fiona.

"No, no, no, it's true," he replied. "This is the best table I have, in fact probably the best table I have ever had." He bustled around taking their orders whilst the sommelier brought their drinks.

"So ladies, you're back with us again and it looks as if you have been missed," said William, once the waiters had moved away. "What have you both been up to during your absence? Something exciting I hope."

"Nothing much," replied Donna. "Got blown up on a catamaran a couple of days ago, but as you can see, I live to tell the tale."

"And I've just been hanging around waiting for her to get back," laughed Fiona.

"I can't imagine how you managed to survive an exploding boat," said William, with not so much as a hint of a smile on his face. Jenny, as usual, said nothing.

"Ah well," Donna replied, "I have friends in high places."

Their starters arrived and were placed in front of them by the ever-smiling JoJo. The food brought an end to conversation for a while as they attacked their dishes with gusto, their murmurings clearly showing delight at their choices. Except for William of course, who managed to find something to moan about.

"Do excuse us," he said, as soon as he'd finished eating, "but I have to finish my lecture." He placed his napkin on the table and pushed back his chair. The others said nothing as he walked away, Jenny scurrying behind him.

"How rude," commented Sue. "He's not even stayed for coffee."

"How come he has a lecture?" asked Win, using fingers as quote marks around the word lecture.

"I guess it distinguishes him from us plebs, who just give mere talks," laughed Alan.

The remaining group enjoyed their coffee together before making a move. Alan and Sue invited Win to join them in their quiet bar, whilst the four women headed towards the Gin Bar. Jess ran on ahead, as quickly as her heels would allow, and found a table. As soon as the other women arrived, their favourite waiter rushed to take their orders.

"Hello, my lovely ladies. You're all looking gorgeous tonight."

"Oh Ryan," laughed Jess, "you are so good for my self-esteem."

"My lady Jessica, you are perfection and do not let anyone tell you otherwise."

"Ryan, why are you in here tonight, you're usually in the ballroom," asked Fiona.

"I'm here for the first few hours and then back in the ballroom later, when it gets busier. The usual for you all?"

"Please," they all chorused. Ryan moved on to the next table, no doubt giving a similar patter.

"Right, let's get down to business," said Carol. "What's new?"

"Before we talk about that," said Jess, "there's something that's been intriguing me about you two. Who is this Angelo you've mentioned?"

"Ahh, well, long story cut short," began Donna. "We first met Angelo in Paris, around thirty years ago now. I was aware of this man who turned up everywhere we went. Fiona couldn't see him and he never spoke to us."

"We went to the police because it was getting a bit scary," continued Fiona, "but they couldn't do anything because he hadn't done anything wrong."

"On the day we came home, he turned up at the airport. Our flight had been changed because the original plane was overbooked. We had several hours to wait but as we went through security, I glanced back and there he was. Fiona saw him too. He just waved and walked away."

"The next morning there was a report in the paper that our original flight had crashed, killing everyone on board," Fiona finished.

"Bloody hell," said Jess.

"But that's not all," continued Donna. "Angelo turned up thirty years later at the end of a, shall we say, adventurous holiday in Greece. He's appeared and at the end of every holiday since."

"When we see him, we know that whatever crime we've got involved in is over," finished Fiona.

"Have you seen him yet this holiday?" asked Carol.

"No," said Donna.

"Right," said Fiona, "let's get down to business."

Donna summarised the content of Matt's latest email. The four talked non-stop, mulling everything over and weighing up the pros and cons of any possible action. It was well gone midnight when they decided to call it a night.

But they had planned their next move.

Chapter 60

A day at sea was just what Donna and Fiona needed, time to recover from the trauma of the last couple of days. But first they went in search of Security Pete.

"Ladies, what can I do for you this morning?" he asked, as Donna knocked on his door and poked her head around it.

"Morning, Pete," she said cheerily, "how are you today?"

"I'm good, thank you." Pete eyed the pair suspiciously; they hadn't just come to enquire about his health. "And how are you, Donna, after the trauma of the past couple of days?"

"I'm fine thank you, it will take more than a little explosion to put me down. Now, Pete," said Donna, pulling up a chair. "An investigative friend of ours has done a little homework on the good Dr Mitchell and all is not what it seems." Donna passed her phone across the desk, with Matt's report open.

He sighed, picked it up and scanned the text. Fiona watched him raise his eyebrows a couple of times, a good sign that it had at least piqued his interest.

"Mmm," he said at last, sliding the phone back to her. "It seems a little suspicious, I agree, but I'm not sure what you want me to do."

"Lock him in the brig until we get back," said Donna.

"I'm sorry, that's simply not possible. I would need to have good reason to do that."

"Isn't murder a good enough reason?" Donna was getting a bit rattled.

"We have no evidence that he did murder his wife, so no I can't do that."

"Can't you investigate further? Or at least get the police at home to do a little digging," said Fiona.

"Our fear," Donna continued, "is that as soon as we dock in Southampton, William will be off and running and get away with murder again."

"But my point is, Donna, we don't know he has murdered his wife, do we?"

"No, and we won't unless you do something about it." Donna was getting irritated. In her mind Pete wasn't giving this the attention it needed.

"OK, OK," he said, raising his hands in a placating gesture. "I'll have a word with the authorities in Southampton and see what can be done."

"Good, but it will have to be quick because we've only got just over a week left before we get home. We'll check back with you later."

"You did get a bit irritated with him, babe," said Fiona, as they left the office.

"I know, and I'm sorry. But sometimes it's the only way to get things done. Come on, let's go upstairs and see if we can find a sun lounger."

Relaxing in the warm sunshine with a good book was heaven. The pool crew were a great bunch of guys and kept them topped up with drinks and snacks from the bar.

"You awake, Fi?" asked Donna, an hour or so later.

"Yeah, what's up?"

"Nothing. It's just that you haven't told me how it was for you when you got off the catamaran."

"I didn't get off the catamaran, Donna, I was pushed off."

"Don't split hairs. What happened next, Fi?"

Fiona eased herself into a sitting position, wrapped her arms around her drawn-up knees and stared out over the ocean, a faraway look on her face. The memories came flooding back; they were still very close to the surface.

"People were getting off the boat and swimming ashore. It wasn't that far really, and the free drinks and snacks at the beach bar were a great incentive. I stood on the beach waiting to see you swimming towards me. I was convinced I could see your head bobbing about on the water as you coughed and spluttered your way to the beach. Then the boat exploded. We saw the smoke first, then heard the explosion.

"I tried to swim out, I needed to find you, but someone held me back. I was sure someone would see you flailing about and rescue you, but nobody did.

"Eventually, a coach came and a nice couple bundled me on board. I didn't want to leave. How could I leave without you? We got back to the ship and were taken into one of the bars. The captain came to talk to us, but no-one knew what was happening. Someone took me back to the cabin and a medic gave me something to help me sleep.

"Donna, I thought you was dead. I kept wondering how on earth I would tell Dave. It was awful.

"The next morning Susannah came and told me there was news. They knew they had pulled two people from the sea but didn't know who, or whether they were still alive. Eventually the news came that it was you and that they had taken you to hospital and you were OK.

"The relief was immense, and I think I might have fallen to the floor sobbing. I wavered between feeling totally grateful that you were OK and terrified over what might have been. I even felt angry at you, for pushing me away when we should have been together. Honestly, Donna, that was probably the worst experience of my life."

"What, worse than being married to Jeremy?" Donna tried to lift the mood.

"Yes, far worse. I don't know what I would do if I ever lost you, Donna. You and my kids are my world."

"Oh babe," said Donna. "We've both suffered in our own way, haven't we?"

Chapter 61

"Do you fancy doing a rum-tasting trip when we dock tomorrow?" asked Donna, as she glanced through the daily programme.

"Oooo, I think we should, don't you? Would be rude to come all this way without tasting the produce."

"They've got an excursion from the ship but it's quite expensive. I'm sure we could find a taxi when we get off and do it on our own."

"Are you sure? At least if the tour and bus is late the ship will wait for us. It won't if we're on our own."

"I know," said Donna, "but we can get the taxi driver to pick us up at a certain time."

"OK, if you think that will work."

"I do, I can't see there being a problem."

"Right, I'm off now to do my talk and then the rest of the day is ours to do as we please." Fiona gathered up her papers and the memory stick containing her presentation.

"Hang on, let me have a quick wee and I'll be with you."

"You don't have to come if you would sooner do something else."

"Of course I wouldn't, I'm always there to support you, you know that."

"Yes, babe, I do and I'm very grateful for it."

Heading towards the theatre they passed William and Jenny sitting at one of the many gaming machines in the casino.

"Hello, you two," smiled Fiona. "Didn't know you were both into gambling."

"I'm not," snapped William. "I only have a little flutter when we're on holiday. What are you two up to today? I hope you're behaving yourselves, especially as you haven't got your men to take charge."

Fiona felt Donna bristle.

"We don't need any man to keep an eye on us, William, we are free spirits and will do as we please."

"Even though you seem to manage to get yourselves in trouble when left to your own devices."

"It's our prerogative to do so," she retorted.

"Really?" he said, raising an eyebrow.

"Yes, really. Jenny, you must enjoy being free of any shackles that a man might put on you?"

"I quite enjoy being looked after by a man," she replied, looking down at her hands, her face flushed crimson.

"More fool you."

"Come on, Don, I've got to get into the theatre. See you two later." Fiona pulled on Donna's arm, guiding her away before she said more. "What was that all about?"

"Honestly, Fi, he really pissed me off with this needing a man to take charge business. Who the hell does he think he is? And she's just a simpering idiot to put up with him."

"I know, but she loves him."

"Stupid idiot. I love Dave but I won't let him control me."

"I know. I let Jeremy control me for far too long, I lost sight of me and it made me so miserable. I will never make that same mistake again."

"Good, glad to hear it. You've changed so much since you got rid of him, and definitely for the better."

Fiona gave her talk to a packed audience and was delighted with the applause at the end. She answered all their questions and then hung around, talking to individuals. Donna watched her friend positively glow and was so happy that she was finally doing something that gave her so much joy.

"You ought to do this more often, Fi."

"What, give talks?"

"Yeah, and do them on cruise ships so we can get a holiday and travel around the world."

"Come on," laughed Fiona, "let's go and get a coffee."

Chapter 62

"Good morning, Mr Mitchell, I wonder if I might have a word?"

"It's Dr Mitchell, and I'm in the middle of something right now."

"This won't take long. I just need to clarify a couple of things regarding your wife's death."

"And you are?"

"Pete Sanderson, Chief Security Officer."

"I don't think there's anything to clarify. My wife had a heart attack."

"Can we talk inside, please?"

"I really don't think this is appropriate. The authorities in the UK will do all the investigating needed when we arrive back."

"Indeed they will, but the more information we can give them, the better their chances will be of concluding this case quickly."

"And what authority do you have to gather this information?"

"Believe me, Dr Mitchell, I have all the authority I need. The captain has total responsibility for this ship, its passengers and crew whilst we are at sea. If he feels that something needs further investigation, then so be it. Now, I can either come into your cabin or you can accompany me down to security. Which is it to be?"

"I suppose you had better come in." William stood back and held the door open.

"Good morning," said Pete, as he walked into the cabin and saw Jenny sitting on the sofa.

"Morning," she mumbled, looking down at her hands clenched in her lap.

"Jenny is helping me with my lecture," said William as he perched on the side of the bed. Pete nodded in acknowledgement.

"Are you happy for me to carry on, or would you like to go somewhere private?"

"No, carry on. Anything you have to say can be said in front of her. As I said earlier, my wife's death was due to a heart attack, nothing more suspicious than that."

"Dr Mitchell, your wife's blood report carried out in New York shows high levels of potassium chloride in her system. How do you account for that?"

"She had a heart condition and was prescribed potassium chloride. We all need potassium for proper functioning of the heart and other organs. Simple as that."

"But her levels far exceeded what was prescribed."

"Look," William sighed. "My wife constantly misplaced her medication, forgot that she had taken the pills and then took more. She probably totally misjudged the dose so I'm not surprised there was more than there should be in her system."

"Did you not think to monitor her medication, make sure she was taking the correct dose?"

"She was a grown woman, she could take care of herself."

"But you previously indicated that you thought she might be suffering from early onset dementia. Constantly misplacing her pills and taking more than she should is hardly taking care of herself, is it?"

"Who told you that? You have no right to judge me."

Pete could see that William was becoming rattled. He wondered whether to push him a little further or stop.

"I am not judging you, Dr Mitchell, I am simply trying to establish the facts around Mrs Mitchell's death." Pete stood up, deciding to stop the questioning.

"One last question, Dr Mitchell," he said, moving towards the door. "Why didn't you call the medical team when your wife became ill?"

"Because I didn't know she was unwell. When I got back to the cabin that evening, Eileen had already passed away."

"But you had already told a couple of other passengers that Eileen was unwell and you had been to the medical centre to get her something for seasickness. Which, I have to add, the medics have no record of."

"Yes, well, I was probably on my way but interrupted. Must have been a passenger wanting to speak to me."

"OK, Dr Mitchell, that's all for now. I will be in touch if I have any more questions that need clarifying."

Pete left the cabin, not at all happy with Mitchell's answers. *Perhaps*, he thought, *those two women might just be onto something.*

Chapter 63

"What the hell was all that about?" shouted William, as Pete left the cabin.

"I don't know," mumbled Jenny, looking every bit as anxious as William felt.

"It's those bloody women at dinner, isn't it? They're the only ones I mentioned Eileen's possible dementia to. Has to be them. Why can't they mind their own business?"

"I don't know, William. Here, come and let me soothe you," she said, patting the empty seat next to her on the sofa.

"Not now, Jenny. I'm far too on edge to be soothed."

"But I always manage to soothe you."

William ignored her as he stomped around the cabin.

"I'll do my special soothing, William," she cajoled, "the one you really like when you need to relax."

"Not now, Jenny," he said again.

"But, William, I can…"

"For God's sake, Jenny, what part of this are you not getting? They are starting to investigate me, and I can't let that happen."

"We've only got a few more days until we're back home, then it will all be over."

"We've got over a week, Jenny, over a week before we get back to Southampton. And do you seriously think they'll let this go once we're home? If you do, then you're more stupid than I thought."

"What a horrible thing to say, William," she said as she started to cry. "I thought you loved me?"

"Oh Jenny, I'm sorry," he said, as he saw the tears flow down her cheeks.

"You do love me, don't you, William?" she asked, as he sat next to her and took her hand.

"You know I'm fond of you, and I didn't mean to hurt you. It's just with Eileen's death and everything else that's going on, I'm totally stressed."

"I know, darling, but I can help you with that."

"I know you can, and very good you are too, but at this minute I just need to be left alone to think. I think I'll go for a walk around the deck, the sea air will blow away some cobwebs."

"I'll come with you," Jenny jumped up to retrieve her shoes.

"No Jenny, I don't want you to come. I'll see you later."

He stood and left the cabin, leaving Jenny alone and in tears.

Chapter 64

Finding a taxi was fairly easy, despite the squalling mass of people vying for the same thing, bartering with the drivers to try and get the cheapest fare possible.

It didn't take Donna and Fiona long to find their ride and within fifteen minutes of leaving the ship they were on their way to the rum tasting experience.

"You will remember to come back for us, won't you?" asked Fiona, as she paid the driver, concerned they might miss the ship.

"Oh course, no problem." The driver sounded reassuring enough, but Fiona was still worried and wondered whether they should have done the ship's excursion.

"Stop worrying, Fi, he'll be back," said Donna.

"I hope you're right. Blimey, it's a bit of a shack, are you sure this is the right place?"

"Yes, it's the same place that the ship is doing. Look, here comes a busload already. Come on, let's get some rum before that lot get in there."

Donna and Fiona walked into the shack. Once inside they were pleasantly surprised, it was bright and airy, with chairs and tables covered in blue gingham cloths. Big ceiling fans kept the place cool and the aroma of coffee and spices filled the air.

"Good morning, my lovelies," said a large woman with a beautiful smiley face. She stood behind a counter stacked with a variety of cakes and pastries. "What can I get for you?"

"We'd like to do the rum tasting tour," said Donna, unable to stop herself from matching the woman's fabulous smile. Good energy oozed from her in waves and her laugh was the loudest and most infectious Donna had ever heard.

"Of course you do," she laughed, "everyone wants to do our rum tasting, it's the best on the island. Tony will take you." She pointed over at a tall, slim man, dressed in bright red shorts, a Bob Marley T-shirt, flip-flops and dreadlocks tied at the nape of his neck that reached down to his waist. "But you come back after and have some of my banana bread, you hear?"

"Yes, we certainly will," smiled Fiona.

"Good morning, beautiful souls," said Tony, with an equally captivating smile. "We have a tour bus just in, do you mind joining them?"

"Not at all," said Fiona, "the more the merrier."

Passengers from the coach started piling into the shack, ready to sample the delights of the rum distillery. Distillery was rather a grand word for the shed that Tony took them into. Someone had obviously cobbled together the structure with pieces of wood found lying around. Probably driftwood washed ashore, Fiona mused. Hundreds of barrels lined the so-called walls, stacked from floor to ceiling, and centre stage was a large copper distiller. The heat in the shack was stifling and the aroma of the fermenting rum was intoxicating. It didn't take Tony long to guide them around the fairly small area, explaining the production process of turning sugar cane into the best rum on the island, and probably the world.

After the brief tour of the shack came the part they were all waiting for, the tasting. Half a dozen barrels lined the exit, and on top of each a different bottle and enough glasses for the guests. A teenage boy poured the rum amid ooos and ahhs as everyone took their first sip.

"Hello, William, Jenny," said Donna, "fancy seeing you two here."

"Ladies," said William, inclining his head. "Yes, we decided to get off the ship today and join the masses in something a little touristy. I didn't see you two on the bus."

"No," said Donna. "We decided to do our own thing and came by taxi." William moved away and it was clear he didn't want to spend any longer than necessary in their company.

"To be honest," whispered Fiona, "I could do with some Coke in this."

"That's sacrilege," said Donna, looking aghast. "How could you ruin a good rum with Coke?"

"Because I can't tell whether this is good or not. Can you?"

"No, not really. But I know I like it."

After tasting half a dozen tots of rum, just about everyone was feeling the effects. The queue buying bottles to take home was long and had Estelle and Tony running around trying to get everyone served before they needed to be back on the bus. The driver had a hard time trying to round up the stragglers, but finally the bus pulled away and Donna and Fiona made their way into the peace of the shack for a much-needed coffee.

"Hello, my lovelies," said Estelle, her gorgeous smile radiating around the shack. "Did you enjoy the rum?"

"Yes, very much," replied Fiona, "but now we need coffee."

"Of course you do," Estelle's joyous laugh rang out. "Go relax outside, I'll bring the coffee."

Donna walked to the side entrance of the shack and sucked in her breath at the amazing sight in front of her.

"Fiona," she called, "come and look at this."

Outside the almost white sands of the beach led down to the turquoise ocean, which in turn connected to the azure blue sky. Not a cloud could be seen. Palm trees provided some shade, a couple of hammocks swung in the breeze, and a few chairs and tables were placed on a covered terrace.

"This is the closest to paradise I've ever been," said Donna.

"You say that about somewhere we visit on every holiday," laughed Fiona.

"I mean it this time. This place is spectacular."

"It certainly is," agreed Fiona. "You would never think this was here from the front, would you?"

"Here we are, lovelies," said Estelle, carrying a tray laden with coffee and banana bread. With her colourful patterned dress swinging in the breeze, the matching scarf wrapped artistically around her head, gold hoops dangling from her ears, and a splash of bright red lipstick, Estelle was a personality larger than life.

"I brought you some of my banana bread to try, I hope you enjoy it."

"Thank you, it looks delicious," said Fiona.

"This place is heaven on earth," said Donna. "I bet you get loads of visitors."

"Not so much," Estelle replied. "We get by, but more customers would be good."

"Do you mind if I take some photos and share on my social media pages? Your beautiful face alone would draw in the crowds."

"Help yourself, sugar, I'll take anything that might work."

Donna snapped away with her phone with countless photos of Estelle, the shack, the amazing scenery, even the banana bread.

"I'm not guaranteeing anything," said Donna, "but it won't be for the want of trying."

"Donna, how many social media accounts do you have?" Fiona asked after Estelle had left.

"Just the one, but I could have more." She sent a message to Matt, asking him to add the attached photos to her account, and give a glowing report of the place. "There, all done."

After an hour of relaxing in the shade and enjoying their coffee and scrumptious banana bread, neither of them wanted to leave.

"I guess we'd better make a move," said Donna lazily.

"I'm just going back in to buy some rum and banana bread, then I'm ready," said Fiona. Donna joined her and with full carrier bags, the pair walked out to the front porch to await their taxi.

"I don't have a good feeling about this," said Donna half an hour later, and well past their pick-up time.

Chapter 65

"Matt!" shouted Jason, running down the stairs. "I've sold a story."

Matt ran from the kitchen and grabbed him in a hug, as the pair danced round the hallway.

"That's fantastic. Well done, sugar, I'm so pleased for you. How much did they pay?"

"It's not much, and it certainly won't buy us many luxuries, but I got £500."

"That's great, and it's a start. Once you get your name out there and build your reputation, everyone will be lining up to buy your stories."

"I love your faith in me, Matt, but it's finding the stories worth writing that's tough."

"What you need is to get a major story out there before it breaks in the news."

"Yeah, I do. Just have to keep looking."

"What about all the stuff that Donna and Fiona get involved in, can't you write about those?"

"I wrote up the last adventure in Singapore, but I've not done anything with it. Trouble is, it all happened overseas so the British press aren't so interested."

"Then try the international press, there must be some organisation that deals with all that?"

"Yes there is," Jason looked as if he'd just had a lightbulb moment.

"The trouble with you, my love, is you're not thinking outside the box. Think big, go global. You're not restricted to the UK, sugar, the world is your oyster."

Jason grabbed Matt's face in both hands and kissed the end of his nose.

"I love you," he said laughing, and then ran back upstairs to do some research.

Matt smiled as he walked back into the kitchen and switched the kettle on. He loved Jason to bits, but sometimes he just needed a shove in the right direction to get him going. Jason was extremely good at what he did and his writing was excellent, and Matt understood that finding the right story was difficult, but he just needed to widen his sights and he would be fabulous.

He took his coffee out to the garden and sat at the small bistro table. As he looked around the large space he wondered if it was time they all thought about how they wanted their gardens to be. Although it wasn't his house, he still wanted a nice space to relax in and it needed shrubs and plants to give it that homely feel. Something to talk about when the girls got home, he thought and hoped that Tom wouldn't mind him having an input into the garden design.

Thinking about the girls made him wonder what they were getting up to, certain they would have stories to tell once they got home. He wondered what was happening with William Mitchell, were the ship's security checking him out? He sent a quick WhatsApp message to Donna, asking for an update and if there was there anything else he and Jason could do.

Jason appeared an hour later carrying a couple of beers.

"I've joined an international freelance journalists' group, and there are several more that look interesting. Apart from working alone, there are collaborative projects to join too. I think it's a great way forward, so thanks for that bit of advice."

"I think if you look further afield you might get more interest."

"I agree. Let's drink these, grab Dave and head down the pub and celebrate my selling a story."

Chapter 66

"Shit, Donna, we'll miss the ship. What do we do now?"

"We'll have to get another taxi, if we can." Donna got up from the front porch steps and went in search of Estelle.

"Hello, lovely, I thought you had gone ages ago."

"Our taxi hasn't turned up and we need to be back on the ship in thirty minutes. How long will it take to get one now?"

"You won't make it," said Estelle. "It will take thirty minutes to get here, and that's if you can get a taxi straight away. It's about thirty minutes to drive to the port. It's a busy time for taxis when the ships are in, everybody wants one."

"Oh God, Fi, looks like that's it for us."

"Wait a minute," said Estelle. "Tony!" she bellowed.

"What?" he asked, sauntering through from the back.

"Get the truck and take these two ladies to the port. Be quick, they've only got thirty minutes to get to their ship."

"But..." started Tony.

"No buts, just move – NOW!"

"Oh Estelle, that's so kind of you. How can we repay you?" said Fiona, opening her bag.

"No, no I don't want payment, just tell your friends that this is the best place on the island for rum tasting. Go now," said Estelle, shooing them away.

Both girls gave her a hug and ran out to Tony's awaiting truck.

Thirty-five minutes later the truck swerved around the last bend almost on two wheels in time to see the gangway slowly being winched back on to the ship.

"No!" yelled Donna and Fiona together, their heads hanging out of the passenger windows and making as much noise as they could. Tony put his hand on the horn and kept it there, determined to get the attention of the crew. The truck screeched to a stop, the girls almost knocking one of the crew over in their haste.

"Please, please let us on," begged Fiona.

"You're late," said one of the crew, sucking in his breath and clearly annoyed that they would have to let the gangway down again.

"Only a little, our taxi didn't turn up," panted Donna, by way of explanation.

"Please let us on," cried Fiona.

"OK," said the man, indicating to a colleague to let the walkway back down. "But be quick, the captain won't be happy if everything's not in place by sailing time."

Donna grabbed the outstretched hand and scrambled on board before the walkway was fully in place. Fiona did the same. They turned at the entrance and waved to Tony, yelling thank you and blowing kisses of appreciation.

"Phew," said Donna, "that was touch and go."

"It certainly was," Fiona replied as they made their way back to their cabin. "Thank God for Tony and Estelle eh?"

"Indeed. Just goes to show that there are good people left in the world."

"Come on," said Fiona, linking arms with her friend. "Let's get ready for the evening and then hit the Gin Bar."

"Best idea you've had all day," laughed Donna, hearing several bottles of rum clinking in her bag as she rummaged for her key.

Chapter 67

An hour later and Donna and Fiona were relaxing in the familiarity of the Gin Bar, trying to put their near disastrous experience of the day behind them.

"Hi girls," said Carol wandering into the bar, her daughter bringing up the rear and chatting to a very handsome young officer.

"Hi Carol," said Fiona. "Have a seat."

"What have you two been up to today?" Carol asked, as she sank into a comfy chair and signalled to the waiter.

"Only nearly missed the ship," said Donna, laughing now they were safely back on board.

"What are you two like?" Carol laughed.

"We'd taken a taxi to the rum tasting place, and asked him to pick us up when we finished," explained Fiona. "Only he never turned up. Must have had a more lucrative offer."

"We didn't have time to get another taxi, so the lovely lady who ran the place got her husband to bring us back in his truck," Donna continued. "It was a hair-raising journey, and we only just got here by the skin of our teeth."

"They were just taking in the gangplank when we arrived, but we made so much noise they stopped and helped us back on board."

"Oh God, remind me never to take a trip with you pair."

"Hi Fiona, Donna," said Jess, as she joined them at the table. "Had a good day?"

"Don't ask," said her mum, laughing.

"Hope you don't mind but I've asked Win if he wants to join us. I saw him a while ago and he looked a little lonely."

"No, that's fine," said Donna. "The more the merrier."

"Have you got a thing for Win?" asked Carol. "Only you've been talking about him all day."

"No, of course not. I just feel a little sorry for him all on his own."

"I think it's very nice of you, Jess," said Fiona.

Win joined them ten minutes later, and Donna pulled a chair over for him.

"Hello, Win," said Carol. "What have you been up to today?"

"I did the rum tasting excursion," he replied.

"Oh, did you?" said Fiona. "We did that too. We saw William and Jenny but didn't see you."

"No, but I saw you two. Or should I say I heard you," he laughed. "I would recognise your laughter anywhere."

"They were just telling us how they nearly missed the ship because their taxi never turned up."

"Really? The same taxi that dropped you off?"

"Yes," said Donna. "We found him when we got off the ship, and he agreed he would pick us up again later. We paid him for it too."

"If it wasn't for Estelle and Tony, we'd still be stuck on the island now."

"Strange," Win replied. "I saw William talking to your taxi driver when we got off the bus. Wonder if he knows what happened."

Donna and Fiona looked at each other and nodded slightly.

"You thinking what I'm thinking?" asked Fiona.

"I certainly am."

Chapter 68

"Hello, William," said Donna, taking her place at the dinner table. "You look surprised to see us."

"No, not at all," he spluttered, the look on his face clearly belying the words coming from his mouth.

"William, I'm going to say this straight, but you wouldn't have told our taxi driver not to pick us up from the distillery, would you?"

Jenny suddenly had a fit of coughing, attracting everyone's attention, which only made it worse.

"Excuse me," she managed, before getting up and rushing from the dining room. A slight smile played at the corners of William's thin lips and he quietly thanked her for saving him.

"Well, William?" asked Carol, raising her left eyebrow.

"Well what?"

"We're waiting for your response to Donna's question. Did you have anything to do with their taxi not turning up?"

"Oh don't be ridiculous. Whatever gives you that idea?"

"It's just that I saw you talking to their driver as soon as you got off our tour bus," Win said.

"Well, I um, I might have suggested that if he was busy the girls could come back on the bus with the rest of us."

"Despite our bus being full?"

"Was it? I didn't know it was full."

"You were on the bus, you must have seen there were no spare seats," Win persisted.

"No, I didn't."

"You didn't think to mention it to the girls, so they knew what was happening?"

"Must have slipped my mind."

"Let me get this right," interjected Alan. "You told the taxi driver not to come back, but you didn't think to tell the girls that they could return to the ship on the bus, despite the fact that there were no spare seats, and even when the bus was leaving you didn't feel it necessary to get the girls on board?"

"Oh it wasn't like that at all, you're blowing this up out of all proportion."

"I don't call it out of proportion when you were instrumental in our nearly missing the ship," said Fiona.

"You're safely back on board now, so what's your problem?" William stood and threw his napkin on the table. "I'm not staying here any longer to be accused of any more of this nonsense."

With open mouths they watched his retreating back as he marched from the restaurant.

"What was that all about?" asked Sue.

"I think there's a lot more to William, and Jenny for that matter, than meets the eye," said Win.

"I agree, this whole business is a bit weird." Alan turned to look at Donna and Fiona. "Why would William not want you both back on the ship?"

"I think it's time to tell you everything we know," said Fiona. "Donna has been suspicious of William since she first met him. Don't ask how, that's a story for another time, but suffice to say that I now take all of Donna's suspicions seriously."

"We had bumped into Eileen a couple of times," Donna continued, "and the poor woman was becoming increasingly unwell and disorientated. The day she died we went to her cabin to check on her. William didn't want to let us in but when we finally managed to get inside their cabin, Eileen was already dead. As we were leaving after the formalities had been completed, I took Eileen's medication from the dressing table and managed to persuade the medics to send the bottles with her body for checking. The authorities in New York also took a blood sample, which came back showing a potentially lethal dose of potassium in her blood. The investigation is ongoing and will no doubt be picked up when we get home. There's a limit to what the ship's security can do whilst we're at sea, but Pete, the security officer, is aware of our suspicions."

"We think that William knows that we are suspicious and having us off the ship would be better for him and Jenny," Fiona concluded.

A full minute passed before anyone spoke.

"Do you think William killed Eileen?" asked Sue.

"We don't know for sure," replied Fiona, "but it wouldn't surprise us."

"Are William and Jenny having some kind of affair?" asked Alan.

"Of course they are, darling," replied Sue. "It's obvious by the way she looks at him that she's totally besotted."

"Good grief, I had no idea. Did you know?" Alan asked Win.

"No, I didn't," Win chuckled. "It's a female thing, they're experts at picking up the signs."

"What about you, Carol and Jess? What are your thoughts around all of this?" asked Alan.

"To be honest, the four of us have been talking from the beginning," said Carol, her arm sweeping in Donna and Fiona. "All the evidence points to William."

"Evidence? What evidence?" asked Win.

"William was married before and his first wife died. Her post mortem was inconclusive, the only anomaly being higher than normal levels of potassium in her system. William inherited a vast sum of money when she died. Now Eileen dies in the same manner and William is set to inherit again. Eileen was a very wealthy woman," Jess told the listening group.

"How did you get all this information?" asked Sue, surprised at the lengths the girls had gone to.

"Another long story for another time," laughed Donna, "but we have friends who help us get to the bottom of things."

"Are you not frightened that William might try to do something to silence you both?" asked Alan.

"The thought had crossed my mind," answered Fiona, "but as we only have one more port of call, his options are limited. Just over a week and we'll be home, so the British authorities can sort it out."

"We might never know the outcome," said Donna with a shrug of the shoulders.

"What a shame," replied Sue.

Chapter 69

William eventually found Jenny in his cabin.

"William, what the hell have you done?" she said, as soon as he got through the door.

"Nothing."

"Don't lie to me."

"Alright, yes I told the taxi driver not to come back. He'd already been paid so it's not like he lost money."

"But why did you do it?"

"Because those two women are meddling far too much in my business. They're always there, asking their questions," he sneered. "I want them out of the way."

"You should not have done that."

"Why?"

"Can't you see, it's just made everyone more suspicious of you."

"What I do is none of their business."

"It will be if they point the finger at you for Eileen's death."

Jenny paced the cabin, arms folded across her chest. She was frightened, frightened that William's actions could land them both in deep trouble.

"Jenny," he ran his hands down the tops of her folded arms, trying to placate her. "Calm down. Everything is going to be OK. They can't accuse me of anything. Just one more stop in New York before we head for home, and that will be that. We'll never have to see these people again."

"You think it's that easy, do you?" her eyebrows raised questioningly.

"Of course it's that bloody easy. You're making this far more complicated than it need be." William dropped his hands and stomped out to the balcony. He'd really had enough of Jenny. Not for the first time did he wonder whether their relationship was over. He really didn't understand the woman, all meek and mild with other people, but then totally uninhibited when they were alone together.

"William, do not walk away from me when we're talking." Jenny followed him out to the balcony.

"That's it, Jenny, I've had enough," he sighed, turning from the railing to look at her. In that moment he couldn't for the life of him fathom out what he ever saw in her. "We're over, Jenny, finished. Your Jekyll and Hide character is too much for me to cope with. I can't do this anymore. Please pack your things and move back to your own cabin. When I get back, I want you gone."

He swiftly sidestepped her outstretched clinging arms and moved through the cabin. Jenny's wailing and pleading fell on deaf ears. He let the cabin door gently close behind him. Walking down the long corridor he felt nothing more than an overwhelming sense of relief.

Chapter 70

"What a day eh?" said Fiona as they walked back to their cabin.

"Certainly was," agreed Donna. As soon as they walked through the door Donna started peeling off her clothes. "Bloody hell, Fi, I am gaining weight at an alarming rate. These trousers were comfortable when we left and now they're tight. I've got to get this bra off and let the girls out." She pulled the bathrobe from the wardrobe and snuggled into it.

"If you stopped eating so much food it would help," laughed Fiona.

"But it's all so delicious. Thank God we don't eat in the buffet all the time, I'd be as big as a house."

"You choose the wrong things, that's your problem."

"No, my problem is that I just love food. How come you're not putting on weight?"

"Because I watch what I eat."

"You never used to." Donna remembered their younger days when Fiona would stuff her face with junk food.

"That's because we were younger then and could get away with it. Now we're older our metabolism slows down and we can't deal with the same amount of food so easily."

"Life can be so unfair," laughed Donna.

"I'll tell you something now that I've never talked about before. When I was a kid I was fat. My mother showed her love by feeding me. I would have preferred cuddles and kind words instead. But she stuffed me with food and I ate it to make her happy. Many times I would try and cut back but Mum would bring me a plate of toast, or a crumpet, dripping with butter and my resolve was gone. I was bullied at school and called names, my time there was just miserable. PE was a nightmare, I didn't want to take my clothes off in front of the others. I'd dodge the showers. I must have been the only girl in school to have a permanent period. I was always the last one standing when teams were chosen, the groans audible when the teacher put me on a side."

Donna was stunned and silently sat listening to her friend's outpouring.

"After I left school and got my place at uni, I swore to myself that I would lose weight before term started. And I did. Over that summer I barely ate, much to Mum's disapproval, and I walked, swam and cycled. The weight came off and I was delighted with my achievement. Not only did I look better, I felt much better in my head too. The fact that starving myself made me ill was irrelevant, I lost weight. University wasn't too bad, we didn't have the money to buy lots of food for one thing, and we were so busy having fun that I didn't think too much about eating.

"When we had to go back home to our parents, the weight started to creep on again. I was bored and unhappy so turned to food. Then I met Jeremy so curbed my eating again. After James was born the weight just seemed to stick and I didn't have the time to think about what I was eating. James was such a demanding baby and some days I just grabbed anything from the cupboard that I could eat one-handed. That's when Jeremy started to make derogatory remarks about my weight and shape and eventually suggested surgery.

"I got a grip, lost the weight and learnt how to eat sensibly so as not to pile it back on again."

"Oh darling," said Donna standing and pulling Fiona into a hug. "What a horrible time you had, I am so sorry."

"It's not your fault, babe, I just want you to understand why I'm so picky about what I eat. I still enjoy a burger and chips, but I'll counteract that with just a salad or fruit the rest of the day."

"Then perhaps you should help me choose wisely for the rest of the trip?"

"I can advise, but it has to be your choice at the end of the day. Your head has to be in the right place before your body will follow. I would suggest you enjoy the rest of this holiday and then work on it when you get home."

"Will you help me?" asked Donna.

"Of course I will," Fiona replied. "But right now I think we need to sleep as we have our last stop tomorrow before heading home."

"Oh yes, New York here we come – again."

Chapter 71

They caught the courtesy bus into Manhattan early. The crowds were already gathering, eager to make the most of their last port of call. Fiona and Donna clambered onto the second bus that pulled up and spent the journey planning their shopping route. They'd already agreed that their first visit on their way out was about sightseeing, this trip was all about shopping.

Fiona was looking forward to meandering down Fifth Avenue and was eager to buy something from Saks.

"Why on earth are you so desperate to buy something from Saks?" asked Donna, bemused by her friend's insistence that they head there first.

"Because I think it has a certain ring to it. Haven't you ever wanted to say, when someone compliments you on your outfit, 'oh this old thing, I got it from Saks Fifth Avenue ages ago'."

"No."

"Oh babe, where's your soul?" Fiona laughed and linked arms with Donna.

"Clearly in a different place to yours. Come on, let's hit Saks."

They toured just about every floor in the shop, and Fiona had a vast collection of shopping bags draped over her arm.

"Please, can we stop for ten minutes and get a drink?" begged Donna. Although she had a few bags of her own, traipsing around after her friend was tiring and her feet were killing her.

"Yeah, let's go up to the restaurant and we can get a bite to eat too."

Donna was grateful to sit down. She placed her bags under the table and picked up the menu.

"Blimey, it's not cheap."

"Didn't expect it to be. This is, after all, Saks Fifth Avenue," Fiona laughed. "This is my treat, babe, I was the one who wanted to come here."

"Don't be silly, we'll go halves like we always do."

"No, I insist. If it makes you feel any better, we'll say it's on Nikos. I've not touched any of the money he left me, and he would be delighted that my first spend was on both of us doing something that made us happy."

"That's true," Donna smiled wistfully, remembering the beautiful soul of Nikos and realising that she too missed him very much. She covered her friend's hand with her own. "In that case, I accept and thank you, Nikos."

The rest of the day was hectic and by late afternoon they had both had enough. Exhausted, they made their way back to the courtesy bus pick-up point and were grateful to see one already waiting. They clambered on board, carefully squeezing their packages along the aisle.

"I'll sit over here," said Donna, "there's more room." Luckily the bus was only half full when the driver closed the doors and prepared to pull away from the kerb. Donna pushed her bags over to the vacant seat and flopped down.

"What a fabulous day," said Fiona, feeling equally tired but buoyed by shopping in New York and her purchases.

Relieved that the ship was still where it should be, they began gathering up their packages as the bus pulled round in front of the walkway. Ever since the fiasco with the taxi, the girls wondered what William might do next.

"Wow," said one of the welcoming crew members, "you two have done some serious shopping."

"Believe me, sugar, we have shopped till we've almost dropped," Donna laughed. "I think I've worn my poor feet down to stumps."

"A quiet and relaxing evening for you both then," he said.

"Oh I doubt that."

Chapter 72

Unsurprisingly, William and Jenny didn't turn up for dinner that evening and hadn't been seen all day.

"Probably keeping a low profile after last night's little outburst," said Win.

"They're certainly a strange couple. This will sound a bit bitchy and I don't mean it that way, but would William really murder his wife for Jenny?" asked Sue.

"We hardly know her, do we?" responded Carol. "She's not said much since we've been here."

"She could have hidden depths that she only shows to William," laughed Jess.

"My God, the mind boggles." Donna nearly choked on a mouthful of food.

"I've never met a murderer before," said Alan.

"You don't know that he is," Sue replied. "But I have to admit that everything you girls have said certainly makes him look suspicious."

"It would make a great plot for a book."

"Are you going to write one then?" Sue looked at her husband with a doubtful expression.

"Might do."

"We'll catch glimpses of Alan wandering around the ship, scribbling away in his little notebook and looking for clues," chuckled Fiona.

"Will he have a magnifying glass?" laughed Jess.

"You may all mock, but when my book is picked up by the film industry and made into a major blockbuster, and I'm an even bigger celebrity than I am now, you will all claim to know me and want invites to the Oscars."

Roaring with laughter, the dinner companions were bonding extremely well. Without William and Jenny draining the atmosphere, the group were enjoying their time together.

"What's everyone doing this evening?" asked Win.

"We're going to the show and then probably end up in the ballroom for a bit of a boogie," replied Donna. "Feel free to join us."

"Thank you, I'd like that."

"We'll be there," said Jess, smiling at Win.

"Sue, Alan, what about you two?" asked Fiona.

"Yes," said Sue looking at her husband. "We'd love to join you, wouldn't we, darling?" Fiona could almost feel her giving him a kick under the table.

"Yes, my little nest of vipers, your every command is my wish."

"Fantastic," said Donna, pushing her chair back as she stood to leave. "Whoever gets there first, grab a table. See you all later."

After the show the girls hurriedly made their way to the ballroom. Win was already there and had secured a table in prime position and had gathered enough chairs for them all. As soon as Donna and Fiona sat down two waiters raced across the dance floor, each vying for pole position. Ryan, their favourite waiter, got to them first. A beautiful grin spread across his cheeky little face.

"My ladies, how beautiful you both look tonight, and accompanied by such a handsome man."

Win looked bemused as Donna chuckled. "Don't worry, Win, he's just after a big tip at the end of the cruise."

"With all this attention, he's certainly earning it."

"We'll have our usual gin and tonics, thank you, Ryan. Win, what are you having?"

"I'll join you both in a gin and tonic."

"Make that five. Oh hang on, Ryan, here come two more of our crowd." Ryan waited for Sue and Alan to take their seats and added two more gin and tonics to his list. He hurried away to the bar.

Carol and Jess were the last to arrive and Donna couldn't help but notice the way Win's face lit up when he saw Jess. *A romance in the making if ever I saw one,* she thought, smiling at the pair.

The music started and Alan and Sue took to the dance floor and Win asked Jess to dance.

The three remaining women sat watching the couples and smiling.

"It's times like this I miss a man to dance with, don't you?" asked Carol.

"Good Lord no," replied Donna. "Don't get me wrong, it's nice to dance with a man, but if I want to take a turn round the floor and my man is not playing, I just drag Fiona up."

"Don't you worry about people watching you and jumping to all the wrong conclusions?"

"Nope. I don't care what they think, I just want to have fun. And anyway, it's none of my business what other people think of me."

"That's such a great attitude."

"I've spent too many years of my life worrying about what others think. As I've got older I've learnt not to give a toss. Life is for living, and as long as I'm not doing any harm to others, then it's none of their business what I do."

"I think I need to spend more time with you, Donna, you have a lot to teach."

Much later, as the dancers returned to the table, Ryan appeared to check whether they were ready for more drinks.

"Let's have a nightcap before bed," suggested Alan to his wife. Sue nodded in agreement, not ready to leave the party yet. The evening had turned out to be the best on board so far. The show was excellent, a Motown band paying tribute to all the best known singers of the day and she had to laugh as she watched Fiona trying to restrain Donna.

"Honestly, Donna," Fiona said to her, "you're worse than bringing a toddler out."

"This is the best night of the holiday so far," Sue declared. "Why on earth didn't we do this earlier?"

Donna watched Ryan moving towards them with his tray full of brandies. She suddenly had a foreboding that something was about to happen, and not in a good way. She reached out for Fiona.

"Fi, something's going to…" She never finished the sentence before alarms sounded across the ship.

Chapter 73

The ship's alarm gave three blasts and then they heard the words 'Oscar, Oscar, Oscar'.

"What does that mean?" Carol asked Ryan. Donna already had a good idea.

"Man overboard," he said, looking serious.

"What should we do?" asked Sue.

"Nothing," he replied. "There are standard procedures for all emergencies on board and it's best that all passengers keep out of the way whilst the crew do their job."

"What about the person overboard, will they be found?" asked Sue.

"The crew will do their best to locate and rescue the person. The ship may stop and even turn around, and the nearest search and rescue will be called."

"I feel we should do something," said Jess. "Someone out there could be dying whilst we sit here drinking brandy. I feel useless."

"Believe me, there is nothing you can do." Ryan picked up his tray and walked over to the next table. The mood in the ballroom had changed and a low murmur began as passengers started talking, keen to find out what was happening.

"I don't feel good about this, Fi," said Donna.

"All her life Donna has had 'feelings'," said Fiona. "Although she doesn't know what, she knows that something is about to happen, or that someone is not a good person. I have learnt to trust Donna's feelings and although I have no idea how or why it happens to her, I fully accept what she's saying."

"Can you explain why you're not feeling good about this?" asked Win.

"Not really," Donna replied. "It's like I know something, but I don't know what I know or how I know it. Doesn't make sense, does it?"

"No, it doesn't," Alan laughed.

"All I can say is that I feel this has something to do with William."

"Oh God," said Sue, her hands cupping her face. "Do you think he's jumped overboard?"

"It's a possibility."

They sat talking for another hour. No news came over the PA system, but they could feel that the ship had slowed down. There was nothing anyone could do and eventually Alan suggested to Sue that they head off to bed. The music had stopped long ago, and the ballroom was virtually empty.

"Good idea," said Win. "Maybe we'll know more in the morning."

Agreeing, they all made their way to the lifts and ascended to their various decks. Donna and Fiona walked pensively back to their own cabin.

"Do you feel it's William?" asked Fiona.

"I don't know whether he's the one overboard, but I feel that he's involved somehow."

"The sooner he's locked up, the easier I will feel."

"I don't think it will be too much longer before we get to the bottom of everything."

"I hope you're right. I won't be totally happy until we see Angelo and know that it's over."

"You do make me laugh, Fi. It wasn't that long ago you thought Angelo was all in my head, now you can't wait to see him."

"I know, but you've got to agree that all this with Angelo is the weirdest thing ever."

"Thing is, Fi, it doesn't feel weird to me. So what shall we do now?"

"There's nothing we can do tonight, but I suggest we go and find Pete first thing in the morning."

Chapter 74

"Morning, Pete, got a minute?" Donna could have sworn she heard Pete groan as she popped her head around his door.

"Morning, ladies, a minute is all I do have. We are in a bit of an emergency situation here."

"Totally understand," said Fiona. "We won't take up too much of your time, we just have a couple of questions."

"OK, fire away." Pete continued to look at his computer screen as he shuffled papers on his desk, paying the girls little attention.

"Have you found the person who went overboard last night?"

"No."

"Do you know who it was?"

"No."

"How will you find out who it is?" Fiona was relentless despite his lack of communication. The one thing working in forensic psychology had taught her was you never give up asking.

"Working on it."

"Pete," snapped Donna, slamming both hands on top of his stack of papers and grabbing his attention. "Would you please have the good grace to give us your undivided attention. The sooner you do that, the sooner we'll be out of your way."

"OK, ladies, you win. Sit down."

"Thank you," said Fiona, perching on the edge of one of the green padded chairs opposite his desk. "So you didn't find the person who went overboard and at this point you have no idea who it was."

"Correct."

"Can you elaborate on that a bit more?" asked Donna, becoming exasperated with his one word answers. Pete sighed again and leaned back in his black leather office chair.

"I shouldn't be telling you this, but last night a passenger reported seeing a person go overboard at the stern but was unable to determine whether the individual was male or female. As you know, the alarm was sounded but it takes time for a vessel as large as ours to slow and stop, sometimes covering a mile or more. The crew adopted their routine emergency procedure but were unable to locate the person. We alerted the nearest search and rescue authorities who joined the search. After a couple of hours the search was called off and we continued our journey. Search and rescue resumed the search at first light. As yet, they have nothing to report. There, ladies, does that satisfy you?"

"Don't be sarky, Pete, we want to resolve this as much as you do," snapped Donna.

"With all due respect, Donna, this has nothing to do with you."

"Technically you're right," Donna replied, "but a crime has been committed on this ship and we want to get to the bottom of it."

"Are you still going on about William Mitchell and the death of his wife? This new emergency has nothing to do with him."

"How can you be sure?" asked Fiona. "You have no idea who went overboard so you can't rule him out, can you?"

"No, I can't. But why are the pair of you so convinced that William killed his wife?"

"You have to trust me on this, Pete, I just know that William is involved somehow."

"How many passengers travelling alone are there on board?" asked Fiona.

"Why do you want to know that?" he asked.

"Doesn't it strike you as odd that whoever they were travelling with hasn't reported them missing?"

"Yes, but it's feasible that if they had separate cabins, the other person might not necessarily know yet."

"Have you checked all the single passengers?" asked Donna.

Pete was losing the will to live. The two women were like a couple of rottweilers with a bone. The only way he was going to get any peace, or work done come to that, was by giving them what they wanted and sending them on their way.

"OK," he said, running his hands through his hair, "this is how it is. The chances of finding someone alive now is practically zero, especially falling into the wake at the stern. However, search and rescue is ongoing. In about thirty minutes, the captain will ask all passengers and crew to check their key cards in at their muster points. It will take time, but hopefully we will then identify the missing person. Once we've done that, the family and appropriate authorities will be informed. That, ladies, is all I can tell you at the moment. Now, if you would excuse me, I have work to do."

"Thank you," said Donna. "See how much quicker it can be when you cooperate."

"One last question, Pete," said Fiona, sending a quick look at Donna. "Why didn't the CCTV cameras pick up anything?"

"I spent most of the night looking at the camera footage but there was nothing. There is, however, a small blind spot at the stern so whoever went overboard knew the best place to jump."

"Or push," said Donna, as she left the office.

Chapter 75

Back in the cabin, Fiona began filling a bag with suncream, a book, water and hat as they prepared for a day lazing at sea.

"Honestly, Donna, why do you have to antagonise these people? You were the same in Sardinia, sniping away at the police because they didn't do what you thought they should."

"Because, Fiona, they don't listen. They dismiss me and my gut feeling as just some crazy interfering woman."

"I know, love, but you must remember they have no idea the way your gut feelings work. It just comes across as you trying to tell them how to do their jobs."

"I am, because their jobs could be done quicker and with better results."

"But you have to tone it down otherwise we'll never get the cooperation we want, and they certainly won't tell us anything."

"OK, I'll try but I'm not promising. Come on, let's go grab a sunbed before they all go."

Spending the day relaxing in the sun was heavenly. The bar steward made sure they had drinks, the outdoor snack area kept them well fed and live music played at times throughout the day. Various quizzes and games produced a lot of laughter and during the afternoon a film was shown on a big screen.

"Are you happy you moved to Angel Crescent?" Donna asked during a lull in the afternoon entertainment.

"Absolutely," Fiona replied. "I must admit, I did wonder whether I was doing the right thing. After all, I'd lived in Oxford all my life; I had my job, a few friends and I also had Mum to consider. But Mum's dementia is progressing, she doesn't even know I'm there and she certainly doesn't know me anymore. I can still visit but probably not as often. It was Steve telling me I could work from home that finally made my mind up."

"What about your friends? Don't you miss them?"

"Not really. To be honest, they're not good friends, they were just people to have a night out with. Since I moved, not one of them has messaged to see how I'm doing. Says a lot, doesn't it?"

"Certainly does. I'm delighted you moved. I love us all being in Angel Crescent, and now Matt and Jason are renting Tom's house, I feel we're complete. We're like our own non-blood family."

"Perfection would have been Nikos coming over for long periods of time."

"It would. You still miss him a lot, don't you?"

"It's getting better. At least I'm not sitting home alone, night after night just dwelling on what might have been. I have all of you to help me."

"You will find someone else, Fiona, and although he will not replace Nikos, he will make you happy again."

"I hope so, darling."

Between reading, dozing in the sun, the odd dip in the pool to cool off and people watching, their day passed in peaceful bliss.

Later that afternoon, they packed up their things and slowly made their way back to their cabin. The lift trundled its way downwards, stopping every now and again to discharge its passengers. At the floor above theirs, Pete got in.

"Any news?" asked Donna.

"Yes and no," he replied. "We've drawn up a list of passengers who have not yet had their key cards scanned, so are in the process of following those up. There's not too many, so shouldn't take long. I can tell you that William Mitchell and Jenny Jones are on the list."

"Knew it," said Donna.

The lift stopped at the girls' floor and just as the doors were closing, Fiona pushed her hand in to stop them.

"Will you tell us when you know who it is?" she asked. Pete nodded.

Chapter 76

"Bugger," said Fiona, as they left their cabin for the evening. "I've left my phone on charge, I'll just pop back and get it. You go on and I'll see you in the Gin Bar. Won't be long."

Fiona retraced her steps and picked up the phone. Just as she let the cabin door close behind her, she saw William doing the same thing.

"Hello, William, are you and Jenny joining us for dinner this evening?"

"Umm, no, we won't be."

"Is everything OK? You seem a little distracted."

"Everything's fine, not that it's any of your business anyway."

"I'm sorry, William, just a little friendly concern for a dinner companion and fellow speaker."

"Well you needn't bother, everything is fine. As fine as it can be after losing your wife and virtually being accused of murder."

"Nobody's accused you of murder."

"You might as well, you all think I did it."

"You must admit that you were very defensive at dinner the other evening, after some strange things had happened to Donna and me."

"Now look here," William raised his voice and strode towards Fiona, his index finger pointing accusingly, a menacing look on his face. "I've had enough of the pair of you. I will not have you slandering my name and I will certainly not tolerate any more of your interference."

Fiona took a step backwards, she didn't like the tone of his voice and he was becoming quite threatening.

"William, I think you ought to leave me alone now, please let me pass."

"Oh I don't think so. In fact, the sooner you and your meddling friend are out of the way the better." He reached towards her and grabbed the top of her arm, dragging her along behind him.

"Let me go," Fiona yelled, making as much noise as she could. There was nobody around and no one to come to her rescue.

William dragged her along the corridor, his fingers digging painfully into her arm. The three-inch heels on her shoes made her stumble and hindered her ability to try and move away from him. They reached a door on the opposite side of the corridor labelled 'Crew Only'. William slowly opened it and stopped to listen. Hearing nothing, he pulled Fiona into the centre of the ship, down a short corridor before opening another door and roughly shoving her inside.

"That will keep you out of harm's way while I go and locate the other problem," he said, as he locked the door behind him.

"Let me out of here, William!" Fiona shouted, banging on the door. She continued banging and shouting for what seemed like hours, but to no avail. No one was around to hear her.

CHAPTER 77

Carol, Jess and Win were already in the Gin Bar when Donna arrived and a round of drinks awaited them on the table.

"On you own?" queried Carol.

"Fiona's left her phone in the cabin so she's just popped back to get it. She shouldn't be long," Donna replied.

"Have you had a good day?" asked Jess.

"Oh yes," Donna said. "It's pure bliss to just lie in the sun reading all day. What's not to love about cruising?"

"It's perfect," said Carol. "I know it's not for everyone, but it definitely suits me. There's so much to do on board, the food is amazing, great entertainment every night and then you can just stumble back to your cabin. Meeting fabulous people is always a bonus too."

"Do you always meet fabulous people?" asked Donna.

"No, not always but on the whole people are nice and friendly and there's always some good conversations to be had. This cruise is exceptional though, I couldn't ask for better dinner companions."

Donna smiled and discretely looked at her watch. *What's taking Fi so long?* she wondered.

The four of them continued their small talk and sipped on their drinks, but Donna couldn't quite shake the feeling that something was wrong.

Chapter 78

As soon as William shut and locked the door, Fiona was plunged into darkness. Eventually she stopped banging and shouting, it wasn't getting her anywhere. There was no one to hear her. She felt around the door frame trying to find a light switch. Nothing. She stopped panicking and tried to think. She and Donna had been in tricky situations before and always managed to come up with some sort of plan. It's what she needed to do now, but without Donna she wasn't sure she could do it.

As her eyes slowly became accustomed to the darkness, she tried to make out where she was. She felt her way around the small space. There was shelving containing bottles and cloths. She tripped on something quite heavy and bent down to touch the object, trying to make out what it was. It felt like a vacuum cleaner, but she couldn't be sure. Was she in some sort of cleaning cupboard? She hoped so because surely it wouldn't be too long before someone came for supplies.

She slid down on the floor, waiting for rescue. She must have drifted off to sleep because suddenly noises brought her to her senses. She stood up quickly and resumed her banging. She found a can on the shelf and used that to make more noise. *Please, please, please,* she thought, *will someone let me out of here.*

Chapter 79

"Fiona's been gone ages," said Donna when she couldn't stand the growing anxiety any longer. "She only went back to pick up her phone so she should have been back by now."

"I hope she's alright," said Jess.

"Do you think we ought to go and look for her?" asked Carol.

"Yeah, think I might," replied Donna. "Must admit, I'm getting a bit concerned."

"I'll come with you," said Win, standing up. "I'm not letting you go on your own, especially as we have no idea where William is or what he's up to."

"OK, thanks. Let's go."

The pair headed straight back to the girls' cabin, but it was empty when Donna opened the door.

"Fiona," she called, opening the bathroom door whilst Win walked out onto the balcony to make sure she wasn't there.

"She's been in here because her phone has gone," she said, looking at Win. "I don't like this one little bit."

"We'll find her," he replied. "Come on."

They walked further along the corridor and stopped outside William's door. Donna started banging on the door.

"William, are you in there?" she shouted. "If you are you had better open this bloody door now. I want a word with you."

Silence.

Donna continued banging. "I mean it, William, get your arse out here now."

Silence.

"He's not in there, Donna," said Win. "Come on, we're wasting time."

Chapter 80

"Ssshh," said Win, placing a hand on Donna's arm. "Listen."

"What am I listening to?" she asked.

"Can you hear that noise?"

"That knocking you mean?"

Win nodded, unsure what the knocking was or even where it was coming from, but he was getting more and more concerned about Fiona and was considering everything.

"It's coming from over there," Donna pointed to a place on the opposite side of the corridor. "There's a door down there, let's go and check."

As they reached the door the banging grew louder. Win pulled it open, the noise coming from within.

They moved slowly down the short corridor, the noise growing in loudness with each step.

"Fiona," Donna shouted. The banging stopped. "Fiona, are you there?" Donna heard her name called and she and Win started opening doors.

"Fiona," she called, "knock on the door again, we're coming."

Fiona was flooded with relief and started knocking again. A couple of seconds later the door opened and she fell out and into Win's arms.

"Oh my God, Fiona, what the hell happened?" he asked.

"William," she said.

"Come on, darling," said Donna, hugging her friend close to her. "Let's get you out of here. Are you OK, did he hurt you?"

"I'm sure I'll have a few bruises on my arm, but I'm OK. Let's go to the Gin Bar, I could do with a stiff drink."

Chapter 81

"You've been ages," said Carol when they finally reached the Gin Bar.

"We finally found Fiona locked in a cleaning cupboard," explained Win.

"Oh my God," said Jess. "What happened?"

Fiona flopped into a chair and took a large swig from one of the gin and tonics on the table. She had no idea whose drink it was, she just knew she needed a stiff drink to calm her nerves.

"William happened," said Donna.

"I'd been back to the cabin to pick up my phone and he was just leaving his as I shut our door. He became quite intimidating."

"In what way was he intimidating?" asked Jess.

"He almost said that we had accused him of murdering his wife and slandering his name. I told him his tone was threatening. He wagged his finger as he walked towards me, saying I didn't know the meaning of the word and I should learn to mind my own business. He had a really nasty look on his face and then he grabbed my arm and dragged me down the corridor. He locked me in a cleaning cupboard, saying he was off to locate the other problem. I presume he meant you, Don."

"We need to let Pete know," said Carol.

"Carol's right," said Donna. "Pete needs to know that William is still on board, and that he's becoming aggressive."

"Sounds like a guilty man to me," said Win. "We can't have him roaming the ship, he could be putting people at risk. I do think you two might be in danger; please don't go round the ship alone anymore."

"He seems to have a problem with Donna and me, so we'll keep together. But I agree that Pete needs to know."

"Pete needs to know what?" Pete happened to be walking through the bar when he overhead the last bit of their conversation.

"Just the man we need," said Donna. "Come and have a seat. Do you want a drink?"

"No, I'm on duty, but thank you. What do I need to know?"

"William has just locked Fiona in a cleaning cupboard."

"What!" Pete exclaimed, eyes opening wide.

"Yes, he was very aggressive towards her and said he was off to find the other source of his problem," Win chipped in.

"Fiona, start at the beginning and tell me exactly what happened," said Pete.

Fiona slowly told the story. Donna and Win told of their part and how they found Fiona banging on the cupboard door.

"He's out there now looking for Donna. God knows what he has in store for the pair of them."

"Right, I've got to go now, but I'll catch up with you later."

"Oh before you go…" Donna called, but Pete was already halfway down the corridor.

"Let's go and eat," said Carol. "There's nothing to be gained by sitting here."

Sue and Alan were already at the table by the time the others arrived.

"Any new developments?" asked Alan.

"Fiona has just been locked into a cupboard by a very aggressive and threatening William," said Jess.

"What?" both Alan and Sue said together, astounded by the turn of events.

"Yes," said Fiona. "It was all a bit scary but Donna and Win found me and after a large gin, I'm feeling much better. I don't want to be left alone though, not with him roaming the ship."

"I should think not," exclaimed Sue.

"Have you reported it?" asked Alan.

"Yes, Pete knows so hopefully he will do something about it."

"We saw Pete this morning," said Fiona, "and although he was a bit off-ish at first he soon caved in to Donna's insistence. At that point no one had been recovered from the sea. Search and rescue were resuming the search at first light this morning."

"As you know we all had to get our key passes scanned this morning and the latest we heard was that William and Jenny were on the list of passengers still not accounted for. The crew were chasing those people," added Donna.

"Now we know that William is still on board," continued Win, "we can cross him off the list."

"So that just leaves Jenny," said Jess, raising her eyebrows.

"You don't think...?" Alan didn't finish the sentence.

"I think it's a definite possibility," said Donna. They all looked a little shocked that of their three dinner companions at the start of their voyage, one was dead, one was missing and the third suspected of murder. A hush fell across the table.

"I suggest," said Carol suddenly, "that we put this whole sorry state of affairs aside for the rest of the evening and concentrate on having a good time. After all, we've only got a few more nights until we get back home."

It was well gone midnight when Donna and Fiona made their way back to their cabin, both carrying their shoes and trying hard not to giggle as they lurched from side to side, which had nothing to do with the rocking of the boat.

"Oh look, we have mail," Fiona laughed, pulling a white envelope from the rack on the wall.

"What is it?" asked Donna, fumbling with the key card and trying hard to unlock the cabin door.

"It's from Pete. He's asking if we could pop in and see him first thing in the morning."

Chapter 82

They headed down to Pete's office early the following morning, eager to know what he wanted. It was unlike Pete to seek them out, let alone part with information.

"Morning, ladies," he said as they knocked and slowly opened the door. "Come and take a seat."

"Morning," said Fiona. "You wanted to see us?"

"Yes. First of all, I owe you an apology, Donna. It seems your instinct was right and I'm sorry I dismissed it."

"Thank you," said Donna graciously.

"Now, to bring you up to date. By the time I saw you in the Gin Bar last evening, we had whittled down our list of missing persons to just two – William Mitchell and Jenny Jones. After seeing you, Fiona, we knew that our man overboard, so to speak, was Jenny."

"Oh God," said Fiona. "Has she been recovered?"

"No, not that I'm aware of."

"She was an odd creature," said Donna, "but she didn't deserve to die like that."

"We can't be certain she is dead yet, Donna," said Pete, "we have no body. However, it's highly unlikely that she would survive going overboard at the point where she was seen entering the water."

"What about William? What did he have to say?" asked Fiona.

"When I left you in the Gin Bar, I went straight to William's cabin. He was reluctant to let me in but eventually capitulated. First I told him that we believed Jenny was the person overboard. He told me not to be so ridiculous, it must be someone else and I needed to do my job properly. He became quite belligerent and abusive, so I called a couple of the security team. I then asked him why he had locked you in a cleaning cupboard," Pete said, looking at Fiona.

"Did he deny it?" asked Donna.

"No, on the contrary. He said that he felt unsafe with the pair of you interfering in his business and slandering his name and that you needed locking up so he could feel safe. He was then taken down to the brig, where he spent the night. I have seen him this morning and he is still professing his innocence. From the evidence you provided, I have reason to doubt him, so for everyone's safety I am keeping him locked up until we dock in Southampton. He will be handed over to the authorities there who are in a far better position to investigate thoroughly."

"Phew, thank heavens for that," said Donna. "I had visions of him leaving the ship and legging it, getting away with murder."

"Do you really think we were at risk?" asked Fiona.

"Yes, I do I'm afraid. He blamed the pair of you for meddling in his affairs and accusing him of murder."

"We never accused him of anything, let alone murder," said Fiona.

"I'm sure you didn't," Pete responded, "but in his mind you are the two who caused his downfall and, to quote him 'you will get your comeuppance'. Much safer to make sure that he can't get to you."

"So that's the end of it all then?" asked Donna.

"Yes, as far as we are concerned. We'll hand him over and it's down to the police to take it from there."

"Will we ever find out what happens to him?"

"I doubt it, Fiona, unless you are asked to give evidence and appear in court."

"Blimey," exclaimed Donna.

"I suggest you spend your last few days enjoying yourselves. Again, I'm sorry I didn't take you more seriously at the beginning." Pete stood and moved to open the door for the girls to leave.

"It's all a bit of an anti-climax, isn't it?" said Fiona, as they made their way to the upper deck for some breakfast.

"This is not over yet, Fi."

"How do you mean?"

"Don't know. But I just have a feeling that there's more to come."

Chapter 83

The next couple of days passed without incident and both girls felt relieved that William was out of the way. Fiona gave her final talk to great applause and fabulous comments. She was riding high on adrenalin and seriously considered speaking on cruises more often.

Donna enjoyed her days lazing in the sun and reading, whilst spending evenings in the great company of their new-found friends. They had already swapped contact details so they could stay in touch and hoped that they could schedule another working trip together at some point in the future.

"I shall miss everyone when we get home," she said, putting her book down by her side on the sunbed.

"It's always the same when a holiday ends, isn't it?" said Fiona. "You form bonds for a short while and then it's over. Look at Julie in Sardinia, we haven't heard from her for ages."

"Yeah, but maybe it's partly our fault too. Have you messaged her recently?" asked Donna.

"No, I haven't and you're right. Maintaining friendships works both ways. I'll message her now." Fiona rummaged in her bag for her phone and started tapping away.

"I'll be happy when we see Angelo," said Donna, thinking aloud.

"What's that?"

"Oh nothing really, just me thinking we haven't seen Angelo yet and how much happier I'll be when we do."

"I don't see what can happen next, Don. William's locked up and the police will take over when we get back. Surely that's the end of it."

"You would think so, wouldn't you? But on every holiday it's never been truly over until we've seen Angelo. It just makes me a bit uneasy, that's all."

"It's out of our control now, babe, so just relax and enjoy the rest of the trip. We'll soon be back home and life will continue as normal."

"Not quite, Fi, I think I've come to a decision."

"Oh, what?" Fiona worried that it might be some ridiculous scheme that her friend was prone to.

"I'm packing in my job."

"Really? I thought you loved nursing."

"I do. Or let's say I did. But since moving to the new hospital I've not really settled. Maybe it's the people, or the different way of working, I don't know. So, what with that and the cuts to the NHS which means everyone is permanently exhausted, I've decided to quit."

"What will you do all day? I know what you're like, you'll get bored."

"I don't know, maybe I'll take up some hobbies, or learn something new. I'll have more time to plague you. Maybe I could help Jason with his investigative journalism stuff. I don't know yet, Fi, but something will come along."

"I suppose so," said Fiona, but she wasn't too convinced.

"Sometimes, Fiona, if you don't make space in your life there's no room for anything new. I think I'm ready for a new adventure."

Oh hell, thought Fiona, *no doubt I'll get drawn into Donna's new crazy scheme.*

Chapter 84

The final full day at sea brought mixed emotions to the group of new friends.

Win wondered why they had all waited until half the trip was over before they all bonded so well. There was so much wasted time that he could have spent with Jess. Meeting someone like her on board was totally unexpected. He hoped their relationship would be more than a holiday fling. Not only was Jess beautiful, there was something about her that touched a part of him that had never been touched before.

Jess wondered what the hell had happened. Win was totally not her type, yet here she was feeling morose that they had to part the following day. She would miss so much about him, his quick wit and humour, his kindness and generosity, the way he looked at her like she was the only person in the room, the way he listened to her when she spoke, the way he made her feel. She hoped their relationship would grow, and she resolved to work hard to make it work.

Carol would miss her new-found friends, but had to wonder whether they would all stay in touch. In her experience, it was rare that holiday friendships stayed the course. Out of sight, out of mind, so to speak. Of course, she would respond to group messages but she presumed it would peter out. Anyway, she had more important stuff to think about right now. With Jess and Win embarking on a romance, where did that leave her and the business?

Sue would miss them all, she had not laughed so much in a long time. Of course, the intrigue with William and Jenny was almost a bonus and gave them hours of speculation over dinner. Such a shame they left it so long before they spent their evenings together. As the oldest female, she felt a strong nurturing pull towards them all, especially Donna and Fiona who couldn't seem to keep themselves out of trouble. She hoped they could all do another trip together at some point, she would certainly urge Alan to sign up for it.

Alan was surprised he enjoyed the trip as much as he did. Usually quiet and more reserved than his wife, he sought the quieter places where they could just enjoy a drink in peace. Sue surprised him when she insisted they join the others in the ballroom, and was even more surprised when he asked her to dance. The evening was a great success, and he was keen to repeat the experience. Plus, it's not every day you get to dine with a murderer.

Donna loved this bunch of people, but then she loved all the people they met on holiday. She was grateful to whoever did the seating arrangements; they'd had the best table in the dining room. Carol and Jess were intriguing, Win was just lovely, Sue and Alan were an amazing couple and so much fun. Even William and Jenny brought an added dimension to the group. It was lovely to see Win and Jess spending time together, she needed to keep an eye on their budding romance.

Fiona felt a twinge of sadness that the holiday was over, and the group would go their separate ways. Delighted that her talks had been so successful, she wondered if there was any scope to repeat the experience. She would talk to Steve when she got back. Hey-ho, one last evening together and that would be that. Her phone vibrated with an incoming email. She pulled it from pocket and gasped aloud as she read.

"What's up, babe?" asked Donna.

"Read this," she said and passed her the phone.

Chapter 85

"We need to find Pete," said Donna, as soon as she had finished reading. They quickly made their way to the lifts, impatient that it was taking an age. Finally reaching his office, Donna knocked and popped her head around the door.

"He's not there," she said, closing it behind her.

"Let's go to Reception, they can page him." Fiona turned and strode down the corridor, Donna hot on her heels. The queue was long, everyone was sorting out their final account and querying every last penny added to it.

"Shit," said Donna, as they joined the end. "This will take forever. Stay here." She ran to the side of the desk and beckoned to one of the receptionists.

"Madam, you will have to join the queue," the girl said in a rather brusque manner.

"This is extremely important, can you page Pete please? Tell him Donna and Fiona need to see him urgently and we'll be waiting in his office." Donna turned to leave.

"Madam, if you'll just join the queue we'll sort out your requirements when it's your turn."

"No, sweetheart, you don't understand. This is urgent, so please just call him."

"Madam, please just go to the end of..."

"I am beginning to lose patience here, so please just call Pete before I get angry."

"Madam, please go to the end..."

"FOR FUCK'S SAKE, JUST CALL PETE," Donna shouted.

"Right, I'm calling security."

"Good, we're getting somewhere at last. Tell them we'll be in Pete's office." Moving away from the desk as the receptionist started speaking into her pager, she beckoned to Fiona, and the pair headed back down the corridor.

They waited ten minutes before the door opened and Pete walked in.

"What's all this about?" he asked, moving towards the chair behind his desk. "I've just had a call from the receptionist saying there was a very angry woman causing a disturbance and insisting on seeing me. I assumed it could only be you two."

"That receptionist is seriously in need of a good talking to and some extra training," Donna retorted, still fuming over the girl's lack of action.

"Read this," said Fiona, passing her phone to Pete.

Dear Fiona

Please forgive me for sending this email to you, but I found your email address listed on the ship's speaker itinerary. I know you and Donna have taken a keen interest in our affairs, so it's only right that you should know the truth.

By the time you read this, I will be dead. I know you will all blame William, but he did not push me overboard. I jumped.

William told me that our relationship, such that it was, was over. He said he'd never loved me, but I scratched an itch. I was angry and heartbroken all at the same time. But it was time I faced the truth. William and I were never going anywhere, and it was time to walk away.

I knew you would all assume that he had killed me too, but you're wrong. I couldn't face a life without William, so I took the easy way out. Neither could I face a life knowing what I had done.

You see, it wasn't William who killed Eileen, it was me.

Jenny

"Phew," Pete exclaimed, leaning back in his chair as he finished reading. "I didn't see that coming, did you?"

"Yes and no," said Donna. "I knew this wasn't the end of things, but I didn't know how it would end. I just had a feeling that something wasn't quite right, there were too many loose ends."

"Will you release William now?" asked Fiona.

"I don't know," he replied. "Like Donna says, there are too many loose ends. It's one thing for Jenny to claim murdering Eileen, but she may just be saying that to save William."

"Agreed," said Donna. "Was she willing to take the rap for Eileen to save him, but thought better of it when he dumped her? A woman scorned and all that."

"But Eileen died before William ended their relationship," added Fiona.

"She had probably been swapping Eileen's medication for ages, hoping that her eventual death would be put down to natural causes," said Pete. "It will take a post mortem to discover the details."

"I guess what Jenny didn't bargain for was you and me, Fi," Donna laughed.

"No, you two were a bit like a couple of dogs with a bone," Pete smiled.

"You calling us a couple of dogs?" Donna smiled.

"No, not at all," Pete's face turned a deep shade of puce.

"She's kidding," said Fiona, laughing. "She knows full well what you mean. But you're right, once we get an inkling that something's not right, we'll keep digging until we get to the bottom of it."

"I think I'll keep William where he is and hand him over to the authorities as soon as we dock in the morning, and let them sort it all out."

"I suppose so," said Donna. "Just seems a bit harsh if William really had nothing to do with his wife's death."

"Yes, but we can't be certain of that. Right now he is one really angry man, and I need to keep you two safe. Fiona, can you send me a copy of that email please? I need to give the police all the background we have."

"What I don't understand is why Jenny sent the email to me and why it took a couple of days to come through. She would have sent it just before she jumped," reasoned Fiona.

"As she said, she found your details in the speakers' itinerary and just sent it to the first address she could find. As for the delay in reaching you, sometimes it happens at sea, they stack up on different servers. Right, ladies," said Pete, standing up, "if that's all, I have work to do."

"Yes, thanks, that's all for now," said Donna, moving towards the door. "Oh and remember what I said about that arsy receptionist."

"Will do," Pete laughed, as the door swung closed behind them.

Chapter 86

"Now what?" asked Fiona.

"Group meeting," Donna replied. "We know Alan's giving his final talk shortly, so let's head down to the theatre. With a bit of luck the others will be there in support."

Win and Jess, Sue and Carol were all in the third row back. The girls hurried down and slid in the row behind them. Donna leaned forward and whispered to Win, just as Alan walked onto the stage to a round of applause.

"What did you tell him?" asked Fiona, leaning over to Donna.

"Developments. Gin Bar afterwards."

"Bit early isn't it?" said Fiona.

"Nope, it's five o'clock somewhere. Anyway, it's our last day so we need to make the most of it."

As soon as Alan had finished his talk, Donna was up and hurrying out of the theatre, Fiona hot on her heels.

"What's all the rush?" she asked, as she finally caught her up along the corridor.

"I don't know," Donna replied. "I can't seem to sit still. There's more to come you know. I can't really explain this feeling I have."

The bar was fairly quiet when they arrived, most passengers either still hanging around the theatre or in their cabins packing in readiness for departure the following morning. They chose a table by the window, pulled up a few of extra chairs and ordered a round of drinks. The rest of the group meandered in, curious to know why they were called together.

"I have received an email," said Fiona, passing her phone to the left for Win to read. "It might be quicker if you read it aloud." Win started to read, his eyes widening the more he read.

"Blimey," he said when he finished. "I never expected that."

"No," said Donna, "neither did I."

"Does Pete know?" asked Carol.

"Yes," Fiona replied. "We popped in to see him before Alan's talk. He is as shocked as we are."

"Is he letting William go?" asked Jess.

"No, he's keeping him where he is and handing him over to the authorities in Southampton in the morning."

"Poor Jenny," said Sue. "She must have been distraught over William."

"Bit extreme to take your own life though, isn't it?" added Alan.

"It is," said his wife, "but that's what love does sometimes."

"Is that what you would do? Take your own life to save me?" Alan turned and looked at his wife.

"No, Alan, I wouldn't. If I thought for one minute you were doing the dirty on me, I'd probably toss you over the side." The group laughed, but deep down they knew it would never happen.

"Ahhh, my little nest of vipers, how I love you," he said, pulling Sue close for a hug.

"So that's it then, mystery solved," said Win.

"On the face of it, yes, but there are a lot of loose ends that need tying up, and I still have an uneasy feeling," replied Donna.

"I guess we might never know the full story," said Carol.

"Maybe."

"Right," said Alan, rubbing his hands together, "what's the plan for our last night together?"

"How about pre-dinner drinks in here, dinner, the show and then the ballroom?" suggested Sue, who was having the time of her life and really didn't want this cruise to end.

"Sounds good to me, OK with you?" said Win, picking up Jess' hand.

"That's sorted then," said Alan. "See you back here later."

Chapter 87

"Oh God, do we really have to get up this early?" groaned Donna as the alarm on her phone dragged them from sleep.

"I think we do," Fiona mumbled.

"What would happen if we didn't?"

"Don't know."

"Perhaps the ship will leave with us still on board."

"Doubt it. Bernard will make sure we leave."

"Why?"

"Because he'll need to clean the cabin for the next lot."

"I wish I hadn't drunk so much last night."

"Me too."

"I'm getting up," said Donna, stumbling out of bed and heading for the bathroom. Twenty minutes later she was out.

"Your turn."

"Go away," mumbled Fiona.

"No. If I have to get up then so do you." Donna pulled the duvet off her friend. "Get in the shower, you'll feel better after that."

Fiona slowly got up and groaned her way to the bathroom, her hair a matted mess and the worst case of bedhead Donna had seen on her.

"Let's go and get a cup of tea and a bit of toast, that might help," said Donna, after she had dressed and attempted to disguise her hung-over look with a little make-up. "We've got an hour until we need to be at our departure point."

The ship was heaving with people when they finally left their cabins. Impossible to get a lift, they took the stairs up to the buffet restaurant and helped themselves to tea and toast. They spied Win and Jess sitting at a table tucked away in the corner, holding hands and looking glum.

"Mind if we join you?" asked Fiona, not sure whether they should intrude in the couple's final few hours together.

"Yes, of course," said Win, pulling out the chair next to him.

"What a night eh?" said Donna, sitting next to Jess. "I'm surprised you two look so awake."

"We just want to spend as much time as we can together," said Jess, looking forlorn.

"That's understandable," said Fiona, "but I presume you have plans to see each other?"

"We certainly do," replied Win. "I'm off to Africa next week on a shoot, but as soon as I get back I'm heading straight to Cardiff to see this lovely girl."

"How long are you away for, Win?" asked Donna.

"Initially three weeks, but that depends on a variety of factors, the main one being the animals we're trying to capture on film. Sometimes it takes ages and we have to extend our stay, other times the animals fully cooperate and we can wrap it up after a few days or so."

"Fingers crossed they cooperate," said Jess.

"Ah darling," said Donna, placing a hand on Jess' arm. "I can only imagine how you're feeling right now, but the main thing is you've found each other. Distance may separate you, but in here," she said, placing a hand on her heart, "you're together."

"We need to get going, Don. Dave will be waiting for us," said Fiona.

The four hugged and kissed goodbye, promising to keep in touch. Donna and Fiona made their way back to their cabin feeling better for having eaten something and the numerous cups of tea. Collecting their hand luggage, and doing a last minute check for anything left behind, they headed for disembarkation.

Chapter 88

The baggage hall was a swirling mass of people. Thousands of suitcases lined up in neat rows, waiting to be claimed by their owners. Fiona headed off to find a trolley whilst Donna found the row their luggage should be in. It surprised Fiona how quick and efficient the process was. In less than twenty minutes they got their suitcases, cleared customs and were outside the terminal building looking for Dave.

"That's the way to travel, Don," she said, "so much better than airports."

"That's for sure," replied Donna, looking down the line of waiting cars. "There he is," she said excitedly, as she spied him about halfway down the pick-up zone, jumping and waving his arms. Rushing towards him and falling into his arms, she realised how happy she was to be home.

The journey back took just over two and a half hours, and as Dave swung the car round to Fiona's house Matt and Jason came flying out of their home to welcome the pair back.

"Right," said Jason authoritatively, "let's give the girls some time to unpack and settle back in." He placed a hand on Matt's arm to lead him away.

"Dinner tonight?" Matt asked, as he turned to leave. "We thought we'd do a barbecue. Gavin, Lucy and Mark are all up for it."

"That's a lovely idea, thank you, darlings," Donna said.

"Great. Just wander out when you're ready, there's no rush. We'll have a couple of drinks first and catch up on all the goss." Jason finally managed to prise Matt away, and they all headed back to their various homes.

Several hours later Donna wandered out of her back door. Jason and Dave were pulling a couple of trestle tables together, whilst Matt bustled about with a paper tablecloth, napkins and cutlery.

"Here's a couple of bottles of wine to start us off," she said. "Shall I just pop them in the fridge?"

"Have you got enough glasses, Matt, or shall I go and get some?" said Fiona, walking over to Matt and Jason's house and clutching two bottles of prosecco.

"You two sit down," he replied, taking the bottles from the girls. "We've got everything under control. Dave, do you want prosecco, wine or beer?"

"Beer for me."

"Cool box is here," said Jason, dragging the box stacked with ice and beer from the back of the garage. "Just help yourself."

"Right," said Matt, as he finally took a seat. "Tell us all about it." The five of them sat around the table, sipping their drinks as Donna and Fiona told their holiday tales. Donna glossed over the exploding catamaran but included the whole sorry saga of William, Eileen and Jenny.

"Bloody hell," said Dave, running a hand over his head. "You've done it again, haven't you?"

"Darling," began Donna, "we didn't do anything. It would have happened with or without us."

"Once it had happened," continued Fiona, "we had to get to the bottom of it. I'm sorry, Dave."

"That's the problem," he replied, "you always have to get to the bottom of stuff. Wasn't there some form of security on board?"

"Yes," said Donna, "Pete is the Head of Security, but he needed guidance."

Jason shot a mouthful of beer out of his mouth as he started choking with laughter.

"Oh Donna, you are priceless," he said, mopping up the spilled beer with his napkin. "I'm going to start the barbecue now," he continued, sensing trouble brewing between Donna and Dave. The smell of food cooking brought Gavin and Lucy from their house. Dave calmed down a little as he went across to Mark's house, calling him to join them, but Donna knew their chat was far from over.

The evening passed and as it grew dark twinkling lights shone around the gardens, giving a magical atmosphere. Lucy and Gavin wandered back to their home and Mark left to take yet another girl to the cinema, leaving the five friends sitting around the table, still sipping wine and chatting in the unseasonably warm evening air.

Donna announced she was leaving her job at the hospital and that Dave was already on board with her decision.

"What will you do all day?" asked Matt.

"I don't know, but something will crop up. I'm making space in my life so that when it comes I'm ready," she laughed.

"What about you, Fi? Any major decisions after this holiday that we should know about?"

"No, Matt, for once there are no decisions to make."

"Good. We want nothing to spoil what we have right now."

"I'm so lucky to be here," said Fiona. "There have been so many holidays where I've had to go home alone, but this is wonderful. I'm so grateful to you, Dave, for building me a house too."

"An absolute pleasure," Dave replied. "This is just perfect, one big happy family."

"Wouldn't it be amazing if we could have some kind of ceremony, joining us all together as family?" said Matt.

"Can you do that kind of thing?" asked Donna.

"Don't know," he replied, "but I think I'll look into it, that's if you're all up for it?" They all agreed that it was probably the best idea he'd ever had.

"Looks like someone has done a bit of gardening whilst we were away," remarked Fiona. "It's looking much tidier down there by the back hedge."

"Oh, that reminds me," Dave got to his feet and headed back his and Donna's house.

"What's he up to?" asked Donna.

"Who knows," Matt replied, "but I'm sure we'll soon find out. By the way, isn't it time we started thinking about doing something with the gardens? Do you think Tom would have any objections to us having input into his garden?"

"I'm sure he wouldn't," said Donna, "but I'll ask him next time we talk."

Dave came back and put a ring down in the middle of the table.

"I found this while I was clearing away some of the overgrown hedge down there. It's a man's signet ring and engraved with initials on the front and the name Joe Parker inside."

"Oh wow," said Fiona. "I wonder who Joe Parker is."

Donna bent forward and picked up the ring to get a better look. As she held it in her hand she became aware of the almost imperceptible vibration coming from it. The feeling she got wasn't good. She quickly put the ring back down and turned to Fiona.

"He's dead," she whispered. "Joe Parker is dead."

Chapter 89

One Month Later

"DONNA!" Fiona shouted, as she opened the back door into her friend's kitchen.

"I'm just here, babe. What's up?" Donna said.

"Read your emails, there's one from Pete."

"What? Security Pete?" Donna looked at Fiona's face and immediately reached for her phone. "Oh my God," she said, after reading his message.

Dear Donna and Fiona

As promised, here's the update on the William Mitchell case I received from the police this morning.

It seems that you were both right all along. William did indeed murder his wife and also pushed Jenny overboard.

The Coroner concluded that Eileen's death was caused by exceedingly high levels of potassium chloride in her system, resulting in hyperkalemia which caused her heart to stop. William had been purchasing potassium off the internet and not only swapping Eileen's medication, but adding it in powder form to her food and drink. His motive was money. Eileen was a very wealthy woman.

The police have now reopened the case on his first wife's death.

After Eileen's death, Jenny became more insistent that they become a couple and marry. William didn't want that and was, in fact, becoming tired of Jenny so pushed her over the railings at the stern of the ship. The area has a blind spot away from CCTV, but a passenger has since reported seeing a man running from the stern around the time Jenny went missing.

As for the email that Jenny sent to Fiona, it was actually from William. He knew that you would become even more suspicious of him so, having access to Jenny's email account, tried to make her death look like suicide. However, due to the ship's erratic internet connection, you never received the message until after William was locked in the brig. We all thought Jenny had taken her own life, but the police traced the email as coming from William's phone.

With all the evidence stacked against him, William eventually confessed. The police have charged him on two counts of murder, and he is currently in prison awaiting trial.

It may be that we'll be called as witnesses, but we shall wait and see.

I thank you both for your part in what became a very eventful voyage.

Best wishes

Pete

"Bloody hell," said Donna, when she finished reading. "So we were right all along."

"Seems like it. Let's grab a coffee and sit outside, shall we? Matt and Jason will love this."

Sitting in the warm autumnal sunshine, drinking coffee and mulling over the case, Donna became aware of someone watching them from the end of the garden. She looked up.

"Angelo," she whispered.

Fiona looked up at the sound of his name. He looked across and smiled. Everything went still and silent as they slipped into the bubble. Just the three of them existed in that moment in time.

"You took your time," thought Donna.

"It wasn't over." She picked up on his thoughts.

"Is it over now?" Fiona asked.

"Yes. He will be convicted, and he will pay the price for taking lives. Thank you for your help."

"Happy to help," thought Donna.

"Will we see you again?"

"Yes, when the next case is over," he continued.

"What do you mean, what is the next case...?" Fiona started but never finished. Angelo was already walking away.

"Follow the ring," he said, waving a hand over his head as he left, their bubble starting to fade.

"What do we do now?" asked Fiona as they snapped back into the present moment.

"Follow the ring, babe," Donna replied, "we follow the ring."

Acknowledgements

Special thanks to Pat who listens endlessly to my ramblings, makes many positive suggestions and has the patience and wisdom to give me space when I delve into my own head. And to Gill for some good suggestions, and some stupid ones, for believing in me, and the kicks up the backside when I need it. Real friends are hard to find and I treasure you both.

Grateful thanks to my editor, Helen Baggott, for pointing out when the plot didn't work, for correcting my many errors, for numerous suggestions, and transforming my first draft.

And very special thanks to you, my reader, for reading the stories. I hope you enjoyed travelling with Donna and Fiona on their first cruise.

To keep up to date with Donna and Fiona check out my website – www.elainecollier.com – or follow me on Facebook and Instagram.

Also By

Innocents Abroad Crime Series

A Greek Misadventure

A Sardinian Misfortune

A Malaysian Misdemeanour

Non-Fiction

Once Bitten, Twice Prepared

The Bigger Picture

All books are available from Amazon

About the Author

Elaine Collier's writing journey begun during the Covid pandemic in 2020, and she has since written two non-fiction books before moving to fiction. Her writing style is a blend of humour, profound insights, and a down-to-earth perspective.

Living in Oxfordshire, UK, she shares her home with family and an exceedingly energetic and talkative cat named Dexter.

After experiencing various careers, including managing her own mind, body, and spirit business, she now dedicates herself to writing on a full-time basis.

Elaine's love for travel has led her to explore remarkable destinations and meet fascinating individuals throughout the years.

When she's not writing, she enjoys crocheting, taking long walks, and indulging in her passion for reading.

She firmly believes that life is a journey filled with unpredictable twists, and she encourages everyone to make it as thrilling as possible.

Printed in Great Britain
by Amazon